HIGH HURDLES

Raising
the Bar

Books by Lauraine Snelling

Hawaiian Sunrise

RED RIVER OF THE NORTH

An Untamed Land   *The Reapers' Song*
A New Day Rising   *Tender Mercies*
A Land to Call Home   *Blessing in Disguise*

HIGH HURDLES

Olympic Dreams   *Storm Clouds*
DJ's Challenge   *Close Quarters*
Setting the Pace   *Moving Up*
Out of the Blue   *Letting Go*
Raising the Bar

GOLDEN FILLY SERIES

The Race   *Shadow Over San Mateo*
Eagle's Wings   *Out of the Mist*
Go for the Glory   *Second Wind*
Kentucky Dreamer   *Close Call*
Call for Courage   *The Winner's Circle*

HIGH HURDLES

Raising the Bar

LAURAINE SNELLING

BETHANY HOUSE PUBLISHERS
MINNEAPOLIS, MINNESOTA 55438

Published by Bethany House Publishers
A Ministry of Bethany Fellowship International
11400 Hampshire Avenue South
Minneapolis, Minnesota 55438
www.bethanyhouse.com

Printed in the United States of America by
Bethany Press International, Minneapolis, Minnesota 55438

Library of Congress Cataloging-in-Publication Data
Snelling, Lauraine.
   Raising the bar / by Lauraine Snelling.
      p. cm. — (High hurdles ; 9)
   Summary: While rescuing Herndon and other horses from a
burning barn, fifteen-year-old DJ suffers serious injuries but also
finds that God has answered her prayer to overcome a life-long
fear of fire.
   ISBN 0–7642–2037–3 (pbk.)
   [1. Horses Fiction. 2. Christian life Fiction. 3. Fear Fiction.]
I. Title. II. Series: Snelling, Lauraine. High hurdles ; bk. 9.
PZ7.S677 Rai   1999   99–6545
[Fic]—dc21   CIP

To Lee Roddy,
mentor and friend.
You have influenced so many writers' lives
and thereby untold millions.
Thanks for the challenge, the push,
and the encouragement.
I thank our God that I met you
when I did—
in the beginning.

LAURAINE SNELLING fell in love with horses by age five and never outgrew it. Her first pony, Polly, deserves a book of her own. Then there was Silver; Kit—who could easily have won the award for being the most ornery horse alive; a filly named Lisa; an asthmatic registered Quarter Horse called Rowdy; and Cimeron, who belonged to Lauraine's daughter, Marie. It is Cimeron who stars in *Tragedy on the Toutle*, Lauraine's first horse novel. All of the horses were characters, and all have joined the legions of horses who now live only in memory.

While there are no horses in Lauraine's life at the moment, she finds horses to hug in her research, and she dreams, like many of you, of owning one or three again. Perhaps a Percheron, a Peruvian Paso, a . . . well, you get the picture.

Lauraine lives in California with her husband, Wayne, basset hound, Woofer, and cockatiel, Bidley. Her two sons are grown and have dogs of their own; Lauraine and Wayne often dog-sit for their golden retriever granddogs. Besides writing, reading is one of her favorite pastimes.

1

I HATE CHEWING DIRT.

Darla Jean Randall brushed the dust off her jeans and glared at Herndon, her Thoroughbred/warmblood jumper. The 16.2-hand bay, so dark brown he was nearly black except for the few white hairs that formed a whorl between his eyes, looked down at her as if to shrug. She could read "Not my fault" in every line of his classy body. He reached forward to sniff her shoulder.

"No, it doesn't hurt—right now, anyway—thank you very much." DJ, as everyone but her mother and grandmother called her, felt like pushing him away or smacking him, but she knew neither would do any good. The fall was her own fault, plain and simple. Riding Herndon took every ounce of her concentration and then some. She'd been so careful to keep him from running out that when he quit, she catapulted over the jump without him. And here she'd been patting herself on the back for finally working well with him.

As Gran often quoted, *"Pride goeth before a fall."*

And, as of right now, her pride was definitely smarting. Her shoulder should have been used to the permanent bruise by now.

7

"Whenever you are ready." Bridget Sommersby, former member of the French Equestrian Team and DJ's coach, mentor, employer, and friend, called from the center of the jumping ring, where she waited patiently.

DJ nodded, straightened her helmet, and gathering her reins, mounted again. "Now, get this straight, big horse: We, that is you and me together, *we* are going to jump this next round with no running out, no halts, and no hesitation. You got that?"

Herndon shook his head, sending his short mane fluffing in the breeze. Ears pricked, he trotted forward at her signal. As DJ had already learned, Herndon didn't hold a grudge for her mistakes. But he wasn't the forgiving horse Major had been, either. Jackie described Major as push-button because he was so willing.

Herndon was anything but push-button, and Major . . . well, after that accident in the show-ring, Major would never jump again. Sometimes DJ missed riding her first horse so much she could taste the tears that she refused to let fall. Major was healing faster than the vet had predicted, but his show days were over. DJ's biological father, Brad Atwood, and his wife, Jackie, had given DJ Herndon in Major's place.

DJ signaled a canter and headed straight for the fence she'd just sailed over by herself. *Three, two, one, lift-off.* The thrill of being airborne for that brief instant never failed her. After a perfect touchdown, they aimed for the in and out. *"Look to the base of the next jump, keep him between your hands and legs . . ."* She could hear Bridget as if she said the words right in her ear.

DJ felt the big horse hesitate at the approach, but she drove him forward. *You have to ride him aggressively. When you learn to do that consistently, your jumping ca-*

reer will really be under way. Since DJ planned a long and illustrious jumping career, including becoming a member of the United States Equestrian Team—or USET, as the horse world called the team—she took Bridget's advice to heart.

DJ's hands followed up Herndon's neck as he thrust off for the brush jump. He cleared it with air to spare and when he landed, snorted as if to say, "See, I knew we could do it." DJ could feel the grin stretch her cheeks. Man, oh man, flying like this was better than anything else in the entire world.

"All right, now repeat the round again just like this one, and then you can put him away."

DJ nodded to Bridget and did as she was told. *Three, two, one, lift-off*. Seven times they repeated the sequence, and at the end of the round, DJ patted Herndon's sweaty neck. "Good job, fella. I get the feeling you thought those weren't big enough to bother with, but we don't get the big ones until we get over our mistakes— before they become bad habits." DJ could feel the sweat trickling down her back and from her armpits. She'd switched her jumping time until after dinner to be out of the heat of the July days. Late July in Pleasant Hill, California, could be hot in the daytime, but it usually cooled off at night. Today, however, she'd gone back to a late-afternoon lesson so she could get home early.

DJ glanced at her watch. "Thanks, Bridget. I gotta run. We're having the Double Bs' birthday tonight. They think turning six is almost as good as ice cream."

"How are their riding lessons coming?" Bridget wiped a trickle of moisture from her forehead.

" 'No fear' is their middle name. They love to ride, and General is one cool pony. He's their real teacher, not me. I just give instructions." DJ wished she could deal with her own fear as well as her stepbrothers did with theirs. She and Gran had contracted to pray about DJ's fear of fire, but so far she hadn't noticed any change.

DJ dismounted and walked beside Bridget back to the barn.

"Are you all ready for the USET camp?"

"I guess."

"You do not sound too sure."

"I know." DJ nibbled on her bottom lip. Should she fess up?

"Something is bothering you?"

"It's just that . . . well, Herndon and I . . . we . . ."

"Are not a team yet?"

"I guess. I don't want to look like an idiot, you know? What if he acts crazy or something?"

" 'Something' meaning running out on you?"

"Uh-huh." Now she did feel like an idiot. "Or quitting like he did today."

"DJ, jumping horses is not an exact science. That is part of the thrill of it—so many variables. You do your best and keep on learning. That is all anyone can ask of you, including yourself."

DJ heard the warning behind the mild words. Learning not to beat up on herself was one of her hardest lessons.

"You will do fine." Bridget patted her student's shoulder. "Remember, you can ride the school horses any time you want. The more horses you ride and the more time you spend in the saddle, the better. That will always sharpen your skills."

"Thanks, Bridget." Such simple words, and yet DJ meant them for much more than the offer of other mounts. No one had to remind her how fortunate she was to have started out with a teacher the quality of Bridget Sommersby.

DJ brushed Herndon down and led him out to the hot walker to cool down while she forked the fresh manure out of his stall, dumped in another wheelbarrow of clean shavings, and measured his grain.

On her way out to get her horse, DJ swung by Ranger's stall to check on him since GJ—short for Grandpa Joe—was at her house helping get ready for the big birthday party. Ranger nickered at DJ's approach, but the horse in the pen next to him only looked at her with little or no interest. Her heart clenched. The white horse that now occupied Major's old stall looked totally out of place. Her best friend should be there in the stall where he belonged instead of grazing contentedly in Joe's pasture.

DJ stroked Ranger's sorrel face before getting the fork and tossing out the dirty shavings. When the horses were taken care of, she waved good-bye to several of the riders in the covered arena and picked up her bike from where it leaned against the barn wall. She flung her leg over the seat and pumped up the rise to Reliez Valley Road. She pumped hard, knowing that her mother would be getting impatient. And DJ still had the boys' presents to wrap.

DJ could hear the twins shrieking with laughter in the backyard when she parked her bike in the three-car garage. "I'm home," she called, taking the stairs to her room three at a time. "Oh, fiddle." Her room wore the transformed look that said Maria had been busy. While DJ usually kept up her own room, this morning she'd been running behind schedule and was barely ready herself when Gran came to pick her up for summer school. The two of them were taking a ceramics class at Diablo Valley College in Pleasant Hill, not far from where they lived. Maria had been the boys' nanny before DJ's mother, Lindy, and Robert Crowder were married. Now the young Hispanic woman was their housekeeper, cook, nanny, and whatever-needs-doing person. But cleaning DJ's room was *not* on her list of responsibilities.

DJ and her mother were getting along better than they had in their entire lives, but since Lindy had become pregnant, sometimes things got a little bit tense. Maria doing DJ's work could cause definite tension.

DJ showered and dressed in record time, glad to be back in shorts after her hot riding pants. Shorts and tank tops were really her favorite dress. She pulled her straight, shoulder-length blond hair into a ponytail and wrapped a black scrunchie around it twice. She'd been called "cat eyes" more than once because of her green eyes, but as far as she could tell, she'd never be teased for being overly endowed in the chest department. She dabbed ointment on a rising zit on the side of her straight nose and made a face at the one in the mirror before switching off the lights and leaving her private bathroom.

When she came downstairs, Gran was helping Maria in the kitchen. Her being there made even the huge kitchen seem warm and friendly.

"Hi, darlin'. How'd your lesson go?" Gran brushed a feathery strand of silvering hair back with her wrist. "Whew, it's warm for sure, even with air conditioning."

"Good. Herndon and I finally got our act together. After I landed on the ground again, though." DJ took a carrot from the tray. "You'd think I'd figure it out that I'm supposed to ride the horse over the jump."

Concern clouded her grandmother's serene brow. "Do you hurt anywhere?"

DJ looked behind her. "Does my pride show?"

"Not that I can see. Cracked pride never permanently disabled anyone."

"How about squished?" DJ waved the carrot and took a bite. "I've got to go wrap something. Need me first?" She glanced out the door to the deck at a twin-sized shriek.

"They're having a water fight," Gran answered before she could ask. "Don't go out there if you don't want to get soaked."

"I'm already soaked." DJ snagged another carrot, grinned at Maria, and exited, a chuckle floating over her shoulder as she headed for the laundry room, where the wrapping paper was stored.

The Big Fib she read on the Veggie Tales video and glanced down where Queenie, black fur dripping wet, whined at her feet. "Give me a minute and I'll dry you off."

Queenie placed a slim black paw against DJ's bare leg. "Ouch, you scratched. Just a minute." DJ leaned over and fluffed the dog's ears. "Now, be patient." She got the foot again. "Queenie, I said no." She finished cutting the dinosaur paper and wrapped both boxes. She knew they'd like the action figures best, but neither of the gifts needed her to play with them. She'd gotten heartily sick of the Chutes and Ladders game she'd given them for Christmas.

With bows stuck on the boxes, DJ finally took a towel out of the closet and rubbed down the wriggling dog.

Dodging the pooch's lightning-fast tongue made the job more of a challenge.

The ringing doorbell caught DJ's attention, so she tossed the towel in the hamper and headed for the front door trailed by Queenie. DJ's uncle Andy held a box that nearly covered his face, and Sonja, his wife, held a plastic-wrapped bowl in one hand and a six-pack of soda in the other. Their daughter, Shawna, who was now the proud owner of the healing Major, giggled around another box, this one wrapped in paper decorated with big trucks and tractors.

"Are we late?" Andy asked.

DJ shook her head and stepped back. "Come on in. If you want to get wet, the backyard's the place."

"Where's Dad?"

"I think he's the one with the hose."

"I'm not surprised." Andy handed DJ his package. "Guess it's payback time."

"Men." Sonja laughed. "Or rather, boys, big boys. I see where the presents go." She nodded toward the table in the family room. "Shawna, over there."

After the water fighters were sufficiently dried off, Robert manned the barbecue while the rest of them carried the food out to the redwood deck overshadowed by an ancient oak tree.

"Oh, look at your hummers." Sonja pointed to the hummingbird feeders that hung on hoops bolted to the deck railing. While some of the jeweled birds sat sipping from the red flowers on the plastic feeders, others hovered or darted nearby, clicking to warn the drinkers away from their posts. One dive-bombed another and buzzed right by DJ's head. She was so used to them, she didn't even duck.

"How come you have so many? We feel lucky to get one or two."

"They like the flowers we have beside the feeders." Lindy, wearing a bright print cotton sundress, might well have stepped off a catalog page for maternity wear, even though her pregnancy barely showed yet. She glanced out across the yard, which had been landscaped to attract hummingbirds and butterflies. The fragrances mingled to form a perfume all their own.

"You look wonderful," Sonja said.

"Thank you. No longer throwing up at the slightest incident makes a difference." Lindy patted her tummy. "Baby here is growing for sure."

"Dinner ready." Maria set the bowl of potato salad down with a thump. "Come eat." After they'd all taken their places, Robert nodded at DJ. "Your turn to say grace, DJ."

When they'd all quieted, DJ folded her hands and closed her eyes. Where to begin? She had so much to be grateful for. "Thank you, Father, for the food you have given us and for our family. Thank you for Bobby and Billy and their birthday. Thank you that Major is getting better all the time. In Jesus' name, amen."

Dinner passed with lots of laughter, and after the table was cleared, Maria brought out a chocolate frosted cake with two round-faced boys painted in frosting. Each wide, smiling mouth was lit by six candles.

In spite of her best intentions and all of her prayers, DJ froze.

2

WHO WAS THAT SCREAMING?

"DJ, are you all right?"

She could feel Joe's hand on her shoulder and tried to answer him, but nothing happened. *Please, God, make her quit screaming.* DJ blinked and swallowed hard. "Who . . . who was screaming?"

"No one." Joe squeezed her shoulder. "It's okay, guys, DJ's not hurt or anything. Let's go on with the party."

"But the candles are all out." The look on the twins' faces showed both sadness and fear.

"I blew them out to help DJ, but we can light them again." Robert gave her a reassuring smile.

DJ looked across the table to her grandmother. *Who was screaming?*

Gran beckoned. "Come on, Darla Jean, let's get the ice cream." She nodded to Joe. "You light the candles again."

"And we'll all sing 'Hap to you.' " Lindy smiled at her daughter and then her two sons. "Hap to you" had been their birthday song since DJ was little and didn't always say all her words right.

DJ forced her quivering lips to smile in return and tousled the twins' hair as she stood up. "It's okay, guys, really. I'll be right back." *God, I thought you said you answered prayers. Both Gran and I have been praying about this, and look what happened. I ruined another birthday party. I'm never going to birthday parties again.* She followed her grandmother into the kitchen, the accusations flying in her mind. The look of horror on Shawna's face made DJ shake her head. Going around scaring little kids, now, wasn't *that* cool? No, weird, that's what.

"And I'm sick of it." She slapped her hand on the granite counter top.

"I don't blame you." Gran turned from the freezer with two half gallons of ice cream in her hands.

DJ swallowed her next comment. She'd been expecting Gran to say something in defense of their prayers.

"Going catatonic like that has to be terribly embarrassing." Gran set the ice-cream cartons on the counter. The others singing "Happy Birthday" drew their attention to the group on the deck. "But no one here thinks any less of you for it. This is a solvable problem, not a character defect."

Her gentle smile made DJ's lower lip quiver again.

"But why, Gran? Why do I do this? I mean, I know I had an accident when I was little." She raised her hand and pointed to the scar on her palm. "But I'm a big kid now, and this makes no sense whatsoever. It makes me feel so stupid." She looked at the splotchy white scar tissue in her palm, then at her grandmother. "I think it's time I heard the whole story."

Gran nodded, then slid the two cartons onto a tray. "Let's go dish up the ice cream and finish the party. After everyone leaves, you and I will have a heart-to-heart."

"Okay." DJ started to head for the party and stopped. "Promise?"

"I promise." Gran's sigh made DJ stop again. Something told her this wasn't the kind of story she'd like to hear.

Both boys looked up at DJ with anxious eyes when she and Gran brought the ice cream out to the deck.

"We've got Rocky Road or Neapolitan." DJ rested a hand on the top of each boy's head and leaned between them. "And you have to choose."

"Can't we have half and half?" Matching round blue eyes studied her face.

DJ rolled her eyes. "I guess. Since it *is* your fifth birthday."

"We're six!"

DJ noticed that they had said "We're six" and not "We's six" as they would have up till now. *When did they start talking right?* They were really growing up. "Oh, that's right, you finally got to five."

"*Six!*" Their squeal made everyone laugh.

"I give up." DJ raised her hands in the air. "How could I have made such a mistake?"

"I thought it was five, too." Grandpa Joe gave DJ a solemn nod.

"*Six. We're six.*" Both twins clamped their hands on their hips and stared from DJ to Joe and back again.

"Well, if you are indeed six, you better choose your ice cream before it melts." Gran held up the ice-cream scoop.

Lindy held up a paper plate with a square of chocolate cake in the middle. "Bobby?"

The boy scrunched his face. "Both?"

Lindy rolled her eyes and shook her head. "Like father like son."

"Yep, I want both, too." Robert grinned at his two boys. "And an extra big piece of cake."

"After everything else you ate?" Lindy's eyebrows danced with her bangs.

"Yep, if I'm going to pop, I want to pop happy."

"He's going to pop, so hop on Pop." The two boys looked at each other and giggled, then said their rhyme again.

DJ reached for her own dessert. But her mind was elsewhere. Soon she would know what had happened those long years ago.

She knew better than to try to hurry things along, so she settled in to enjoy the party. She and Shawna shared a bench seat and scooted closer together so they could talk in spite of the noise around them from the boys' opening their gifts.

In between the squeals and laughter, Shawna leaned even closer to DJ. "Bridget said I could start riding Major next week since I'm so light."

DJ swallowed. "Th-that's great." How she missed her Major. Even though she saw him nearly every day, not having him at the Academy barns made it harder. In her heart she knew his being on pasture was the best thing for him, but still . . . life changed so much, so fast sometimes.

"You . . . you don't mind, do you?"

Shawna was entirely too perceptive for DJ's own good.

DJ shook her head, and the smile she gave her cousin came from her heart. "Shawna, I gave Major to you so that he could feel useful and you could have a good horse and friend. I know that was the best thing for us all, but I really miss him. So sometimes, if I get down about it, just ignore me, okay?"

"But you have Herndon."

"I know." *And one of these days he and I will be the kind of team Major and I were, if it kills me.* She made herself change the thought. *If it takes every bit of strength I own.*

"He's really a cool horse. Watching you jump him gives me goose bumps."

"It gives me a sore shoulder—not watching him but jumping." DJ rubbed her right shoulder and winced when she hit the sorest spot. "If I didn't hit the ground so often, I'd be fine." She looked up at a shout from the twins.

"Thank you, DJ." The boys waved her gifts in the air.

"You're welcome."

"*The B-i-g F-i-b.*" Bobby sounded out the video title. "*The Big Fib.*" He swapped high fives with his dad.

All the while DJ watched the present opening, laughing and calling out teasing comments, her mind kept flitting back to Gran and the coming story. Was the story really so terrible that no one had dared tell her? Or had they forgotten, thinking it not important enough? Why couldn't she remember what had happened? After all, it was *her* hand that had been burned.

Queenie sat down at her side and rested her chin on DJ's thigh, her eyes pleading for DJ's hand to begin moving. DJ smiled down at the black dog.

"You know how to get your point across, don't you?" She began rubbing the dog's ears, causing a sigh of bliss.

Shawna shook her head, chuckling at the dog. "Dad said we could get a dog and Mom said we could get a cat, so pretty soon I'll have all kinds of pets." She reached over and smoothed the fur on Queenie's back. "She is so silky."

"Yep, the boys gave her a bath yesterday. I think they got wetter than the dog."

At her mother's nod, DJ got to her feet and began gathering up the wrapping paper and ribbons.

"Save the ribbons," Gran said, reaching for a multi-colored bunch of curling ribbon. "These are much too pretty to throw away."

Joe groaned. "Mel, the saver. Good thing we have a big house."

"Takes one to know one. Dad, you are the original pack rat." Andy handed Gran another bow. "Used to drive Mom nuts."

DJ watched her grandmother's face. Did it bother her to hear about Joe's deceased wife?

"Getting him to throw something away is like pulling teeth." Gran dropped a kiss on Joe's receding hairline. "But that's his only fault, and you really can't call saving a fault. Actually, *thrifty* is a better word."

Joe snagged her around the waist and drew her to his side. "This woman can turn anything into a compliment, so watch your mouth, young man."

Robert shook his head. "Watch out, Andy. He might be older, but he's still bigger than you. And retired cops know all kinds of sneaky tricks to get their own way."

DJ leaned on the back of her mother's chair, receiving a smile full of love from Lindy. Since DJ had been an "only" for so many years, the teasing that went on in this big new family of hers made her laugh both inside and out. Pretty soon Gran and Joe would have been married a year. Her mother and Robert were married on Valentine's Day. Such a year of changes.

After the mess was cleaned up and the boys had carried their new toys and clothes to their room, the guests gathered up their things and made their way out the front door. DJ got hugs along with the rest, even though Andy's family now lived only a couple of miles away. They had bought DJ's old house.

"See ya tomorrow, 'kay?" Shawna lingered behind her folks. She rolled her lips together. "Would you . . . I mean, do you have time to . . ."

"To what?" DJ stuck her hands in her back pockets.

"To be with me when I ride Major tomorrow?"

"Sure. If you wait until afternoon. Gran and I have class in the morning."

"Good." Shawna beamed. "I know I've ridden him before but . . . this is different." Her eyes darkened in concern. "This . . . it won't make you feel bad, will it?"

DJ shook her head. "Nope."

"Come on, Shawna. You can talk tomorrow." Andy waved from the car.

"See ya. Thanks, DJ." Shawna turned and trotted down the curving walk.

"I think we have a major case of hero worship there." Joe put his arms around DJ and gave her a hug.

"And I think it's good for both of them." Gran looped her hand through her husband's crooked arm. "Maria made a fresh pot of coffee if you want some." Together they turned and followed Robert and Lindy back to the kitchen.

"DJ, you want something to drink?" Gran poured herself a cup of coffee from the carafe on the counter.

DJ shook her head. Now was the time. Did she want to hear the story or not?

"Okay, let's go on out to the gazebo, then." Gran took DJ's arm. "I saw the new cushions on the seats. Should be a good place to watch the sunset, right?"

DJ felt like running the other way.

"DJ, can you play Candyland with us?" The twins materialized at her side.

"Not now. I get DJ for a while." Gran smiled down at the boys.

"But we—"

"Come on, your dad and I will play." Lindy reached for the boys' hands. "And I get the red marker."

The breeze that ruffled the oak leaves lifted the tendrils of hair from DJ's neck. The grass felt cool on her bare feet and invited her to sit. But DJ and Gran continued on to the redwood gazebo Robert had built for Lindy on the far side of the lawn.

"My, this place is so different since Robert got going on it." Gran leaned over to smell a coral-colored rose. "When I think back to all the work you and I did on the yard at our other house . . ." She smiled at her granddaughter. "You've always been such a good helper."

"I like working in the yard with you. Mom is trying, but it isn't the same. You know so much about all the flowers and she's just learning, I guess. Besides, here the gardener does a lot of the work and she kind of supervises."

"Makes a difference. But then, you don't have much time to dig in the dirt anymore." Gran settled back on the flowered cushions, propping one behind her back. "Ah, now, this is the life. I've always wanted a gazebo."

"So tell GJ and he'll make you one."

"I know." A gentle smile teased the corner of her mouth. "He spoils me something awful."

DJ arranged a nest out of a couple of cushions at her grandmother's feet and made herself comfortable. Laughter from the game players sounded far away. General nickered from his paddock, and Queenie's toenails clicked across the flooring. She sighed as she joined DJ on the cushions.

DJ waited, still not sure if she wanted to hear this or not.

Gran set her coffee mug on the railing and used that hand to stroke DJ's hair. After a peaceful pause, she began. "You were only two and such a busy little person, we could hardly keep up with you. I was at work—that was before I got to stay home and illustrate full time. Lindy had gone back to finish school, and Grandpa was taking care of you. He was on swing shift then, so he could be at home with you. We didn't use day care very often. The three of us took turns making sure you were cared for."

DJ swallowed. "So . . ." She cleared her throat. "So then what happened?"

"It's so long ago, I have to think hard to remember all the things." Gran took a sip of her coffee and set the mug back down.

"Anyway, since you were down for a nap, Grandpa had a fire going out in the backyard to burn some brush. He had gone behind the garage for something and was just coming back. Somehow you had gotten out of your crib, opened the door, and toddled out to the fire. Who knows why, maybe because of the bright colors, but you grabbed a piece of burning wood. He said you let out a scream that could have wakened the dead. Grandpa rushed over, grabbed you up, and stuck your hand in a bucket of water he'd kept by the fire. Then he took you to the urgent care center not far from our house."

Gran shook her head. "He couldn't forgive himself. The next night he had the heart attack and died before the ambulance could get there."

"So you're saying I killed my grandfather."

"Darla Jean Randall, that is not what I'm saying at all! Your getting burned was an accident, pure and simple, and had nothing to do with his heart attack. Besides, it wasn't your fault he couldn't forgive himself." Gran leaned forward and tilted DJ's chin up with one finger. "That reaction is exactly why I've hesitated to tell you the story before now. You have a tendency to think everything that goes wrong is your fault."

"But could something like that cause a person to have a heart attack?"

Gran kept on shaking her head. "DJ, when God says it's time for someone to go home to heaven, there is nothing we can do to stop that. Even if the paramedics had gotten there sooner, it wouldn't have helped. His heart just quit. The heart trouble had to have been building for some time—we just didn't know it."

DJ stared at the scar in her hand. "And that's what makes me turn into a zombie when I see fire? I mean, it wasn't like the end of the world or anything."

"The human mind is a mystery. A doctor I asked about it said that the pain of the burn, the fire, and your grandfather being so upset probably all combined to affect you this way since you were so little. But I know that God can heal minds as well as burns, so we will keep praying."

"I guess." DJ kept her thoughts to herself. *How come He hasn't done anything so far? We've been praying.* "You s'pose the voice I hear screaming is really me back when it happened?"

"I wouldn't be at all surprised."

DJ leaned her head on Gran's knee and relaxed under her grandmother's ministering fingers.

"Darla Jean, darlin', listen to me and listen carefully." Gran leaned forward, her elbows resting on her knees.

DJ turned so she could see her grandmother's face.

"God's timing isn't our timing, and He isn't there to give us everything we ask for right when we ask. He *will* heal you, inside and out, in *His* time. Our job is to be faithful in prayer and thank Him for all He has done and will do. Do you understand?" She cupped DJ's cheeks in her gentle hands.

DJ nodded. "I guess. But it's hard to keep praying for something when nothing happens."

"I know, but that's how faith grows. Like a muscle, it has to stretch with use and get stronger. God is in the faith-stretching business so we can become the people He wants us to be."

DJ could feel the sigh start down about her toenails and work its way up. "But it's so hard."

Gran chuckled. "I know, darlin', I know."

I wish I knew what it would take to get over this, DJ thought later. *I just wish I knew.*

3

"THANKING GOD FOR SOMETHING that hasn't happened yet feels dumb." DJ continued their discussion from the evening before on Wednesday morning.

Gran chuckled and turned her blinker on for the turn into the Diablo Valley College parking lot. Their final pottery class started in fifteen minutes.

"I'm sure He has already put things into motion for you. You just can't see the results yet. One of my favorite verses says something like 'Before you call, I will answer.'"

"Huh?" One eyebrow quirked toward her hairline.

"I've seen it happen many times. I will ask for something, but for me to receive what I'd asked for, He had to have started the process long before. Like for you now with Herndon. How old is Herndon?"

"Twelve."

"And how long has Jackie had him?"

"Five, six years, somewhere in there."

"See what I mean?"

DJ nibbled on her bottom lip. "How can He do that?"

Gran shrugged. "He's God, that's how."

"But . . ."

"But what?" Gran swung the car into a parking slot and turned off the motor. She turned her head to watch her granddaughter.

DJ studied the ragged cuticle on her right thumb. Normally she would want to chew it off, but this time she wasn't even tempted. She looked from her thumb to her grandmother. "I didn't want to chew it." She held up her thumb. "Gran, I didn't want to chew it!" Her voice rose along with the words.

"And how long ago did we start praying for you to quit chewing your fingernails?"

"I don't know. A long time—last fall I think." DJ continued shaking her head, all the while staring at her thumb. "You have any hand lotion?"

"Um-hum. And a bitty scissors that can snip that skin off so it doesn't tear further." Gran dug in her purse and brought out both things.

DJ cut off the skin and handed the scissors back. "You have a hammer in there, too?"

Gran raised one eyebrow. "No, why?"

DJ tossed the now closed tube of hand lotion back to her and grinned. "Just checking. I was beginning to think you carried everything in there." She pointed to the straw tote taking up most of the seat between them.

"Smart aleck." But the smile on Gran's face said far more to DJ than the words. Together they walked up the concrete walk, around the corner of the building, and up the stairs.

"I hope that vase I did for Mom turns out as nice as I see it in my head."

"The form was lovely. Mr. Charles told you that himself."

"I know, but sometimes the glazes do funny things."

All the students were gathered around the pieces that had been through the latest firing. Mr. Charles, the instructor, was making comments about each piece. He pointed out both flaws and good points, keeping people laughing while he spoke.

When he got to DJ's two pieces, he held up the vase. "Now, this is the first piece that DJ was able to get above flat or slightly rounded. Not for lack of trying, mind you."

Everyone groaned along with DJ.

"However, she did make some nice flat platters, if you recall."

One of them had blown up in the kiln, so DJ shook her head.

"But this one is lovely." He turned it carefully so everyone could see, using his finger to trace the pattern she'd cut into the damp clay. "And the glaze turned out well, too. Only a bit of bubbling here at the bottom but not something that detracts too much from the piece. Good job, DJ."

Next he picked up Gran's bowl. When he held it up, everyone could see the slight sag on one side. "More work on the wheel will overcome this, but the coloring is good. It should be, considering this lady makes her living as an illustrator of children's books. There is real art in this family's gene pool."

After he'd handed out all the pieces and identified which ones he thought might sell in the show, he came over to where DJ and Gran were glazing their last pieces to be fired later and picked up when done.

"You know, DJ, you're about the youngest student I've had." He studied her choice of glazes and nodded.

"For one so young you have a great deal of patience and a good eye for form. Your grandmother says you are an exceptional artist, mostly with pencil."

"She's prejudiced." DJ studied the bowl in front of her. "Guess this could make a good dog dish if it doesn't turn out like I want."

"What if you added an overglaze that drips down the sides just a bit?"

DJ did as he suggested and wanted to clap her hands for joy. She didn't think she'd use it for a dog dish after all.

DJ glanced up at him. "Thank you." As he went on to the next student, what he had said at first finally sank into her mind. Mr. Charles had given her a compliment, a really good compliment.

And she'd been so focused on what she was doing, she'd almost missed it. Ah well, maybe she'd learned something about focus after all.

Now if she could just apply such intense concentration to Herndon.

But I do, she said to herself. *I really do*.

"You look like the cat that ate the canary," Gran said when they returned to the car after class.

DJ gave a hop and a skip. When she told Gran what Mr. Charles had said, Gran nodded.

"I thought he was a good teacher, but now I know he's an exceptional one."

DJ stopped in the motion of opening the car door. "Why?"

"Because he recognized great talent in the making,

that's why." Gran winked and slid into her seat.

"Gr-a-a-n."

"You hungry?" Gran asked as they turned onto Contra Costa Boulevard.

"Starved."

"Good. So am I. I'll call Joe and tell him we're stopping for lunch, then you can call your mother." Gran reached for the cell phone plugged into the cigarette lighter. "On second thought, you call Joe. I hate to use the phone while I'm driving."

DJ made the phone calls and hung up. "We can't be too long. Shawna is grooming Major, and then they're going to lunge him. I promised I'd be there to watch her ride this first time."

"Fast food it is. Take your pick; there's about every kind imaginable along this strip."

"Mexican."

By the time they ate and arrived back at Gran's, Joe and Shawna were just saddling Major. DJ got out of the car and whistled. Major answered her with a whinny and tossed his head.

"Easy, fella." DJ trotted out to the pasture gate on the other side of the garage. "Sorry, Shawna. I hope he didn't break your eardrums." Major shook his head and nosed her pockets, then looked at her like something was wrong. He snuffled again and nudged her with his nose.

"Sorry, old man, but I just came from class. I didn't need carrots there." She stroked his nose and rubbed up around his ears, turning so he could drape his head over her shoulder. "He likes to be petted like this. This is his favorite spot." DJ showed Shawna the spot inside his ears, almost at the tip. "Feel that little nub?"

Shawna nodded. "I never knew that before. He sure does like horse cookies, though. Dad says we ought to buy stock in the feed company." She dug in her pocket and pulled out a couple of large crumbs. "Here." She dribbled them into DJ's hand. "Now you have something for him."

Major whiskered her hand for more and lipped a trail up her arm.

"Eww, horse slobber. Thanks a bunch." DJ rubbed it off on his neck. "You ready to ride, old man?" Major blew in her face and rubbed his forehead on the front of her T-shirt. She petted him a bit more, then looked at Shawna. "You ready?"

"Am I ever."

DJ checked the saddle girth and turned to her cousin. "Up you go, then."

Shawna gathered her reins and, taking hold of the pommel and cantle of the saddle, put her foot in the stirrup and swung aboard. Major turned to sniff her boot, then looked at DJ as if to say, "What are you doing on the ground? I thought you mounted."

DJ swallowed quick and blinked more than once. Major was no longer her horse. He belonged to Shawna now and had to start becoming her friend. She stepped back. "Are your stirrups all right?"

Shawna rose in the saddle. "Uh-huh."

"Good, then just walk him around the fence line."

Major looked at her one more time before responding to Shawna's signal, then walked out like he'd never been injured at all, his stride as free-swinging as ever.

Maybe I gave up on him too soon. The thought felt like an arrow in her heart.

"You did the right thing." Joe came to stand beside her.

"How did you know what I was thinking?" She blinked back the tears that burned behind her eyes.

"Your face is easier to read than a book—with big print." Joe laid a hand on her shoulder. "He can't jump again. The strain might cripple him permanently. You know how many times that shoulder heated up on you. You need a horse that can go where you want to go, and Herndon can."

"I know, but Major . . . Major is really special."

"You think I don't know that? He was my horse first, remember. For six years he carried me about the streets of San Francisco. I know what a trooper he is, and if I'd had to sell him to someone I didn't know or leave him with the police force, why . . ." Joe shook his head. "That doesn't bear thinking about."

"Thanks, GJ." DJ stepped closer to the fence. "Come on, Shawna, don't let him go to sleep on you. Shorten your reins and squeeze with your legs." After they'd gone a few more paces, she added, "That's right."

Shawna rode Major around the field several times, her smile about to split her face. "Isn't he awesome?" She stopped in front of DJ and Joe.

"He sure is." DJ stroked the white blaze on Major's face. "But that's probably enough for this first time. Ride him only at a walk each day, and after a week, if there is no heat in that shoulder, you can trot him."

While Shawna dismounted, Joe whispered in DJ's ear, "She might just as well move in with us, much as she's here. Major hasn't been brushed this much since you first got him."

DJ nodded. "Good. That's the way it should be." She

explored Major's injured shoulder with gentle fingers but found no sign of heat or swelling. "I better get on home or the Double Bs will be out looking for me. Today Bobby's riding lesson is first. They take turns, and I better not forget which day is which or I'm in deep trouble."

"Not that they wouldn't let you know." Joe swung the gate shut behind Major as Shawna led him back to his stall.

"At the top of their lungs. See ya later." DJ jogged out the driveway and up the road to her house. With only three houses in between, it wasn't far enough to even make her puff. She continued on through the silent house to the backyard, where she realized the shrieking was coming from the barn. Even Queenie wasn't around. DJ let herself out through the redwood gate and strolled down the path to the four-stall barn Robert had built. It opened onto a fenced pasture with more grass than one pony could keep grazed down. As it was, General had put on weight, but with the boys riding more, DJ knew that would wear off.

She turned the corner of the barn to see her mother dodging spray from the hose held by two laughing twin boys. Lindy's hair hung in wet strings, and her T-shirt clung to her body as she dove for the boys. She tickled them until they dropped the hose and ran off, Lindy in hot pursuit until she was jerked to a stop by the end of the hose. Queenie leaped and barked after the boys until they fell giggling in the knee-deep grass.

General stood over at the fence line, watching the crazy humans like a spectator at a ball game.

"Hi." DJ strolled out to where her mother was taking a drink from the hose.

"Hi, yourself. How was class?" Lindy pushed her hair back behind one ear.

"Great. Mr. Charles said I had a good eye for form and worked well with clay."

"Wow! That's neat."

The boys jumped in place and waved hands at their mother, coming closer one step at a time.

Lindy brandished the hose at them, and they ran backward till they fell down again. Gran could probably hear their screams and laughing all the way over at her house. "You look hot."

"Sure. It's hot out, and I ran home so I could be here for the boys' lessons."

"Ah." Lindy got a gleam in her eye and glanced down at the hose in her hand.

"Oh no, don't you do it." DJ backpedaled but not nearly fast enough. Like a snake striking, Lindy pointed the hose at DJ, thumbing the end of it so the spray followed the retreating girl.

"M-o-t-h-e-r!"

"Get DJ, get her again!" one of the twins squealed.

With a dive, DJ cranked the hose bib and shut the water off. She shook the water from her hair and backhanded the streams running down her face and onto her shirt. She pulled the shirt out from her body, all the while shaking her head. "I can't believe this. Drowned by my own mother."

The boys ran to her side, laughing up at her. "You're wet."

"You're all wet," said the other.

"We were giving General a bath."

"Looks to me like you are wetter than the horse." Now that they mentioned it, DJ noticed the pony's mane hung in damp strings. "And so is Queenie." DJ looked again at her mother. Shaking her head was getting to be a habit in regard to her used-to-be perfectly groomed and reserved mother. "And me."

"Now I know that the tales you used to tell about water fights on the wash rack are all true." Lindy dug in her pocket and pulled out a scrunchie. Smoothing her hair back from her face, she bound it in back and took in a deep breath. "They say that laughing is one of the best forms of exercise, and I tell you, we got our share in today." She gathered the boys to her sides and shrugged. "Must be good for the baby, don't you think?"

"I guess. You two go on up and put on dry pants so you don't stick to the saddle, okay? I'll get General tacked up."

The boys ran to the house yelling "Race you" and "I won" and "No, I did."

Lindy rolled her eyes. "Wish I could bottle all that energy. We'd be wealthy beyond measure." She strolled with DJ out to General and took hold of his halter. "He sure is a good-natured creature, not like I'd heard ponies were at all."

"People tend to think all ponies are like the bad-tempered, stubborn Shetlands. General has enough Arab in him to be more like a horse. Welsh ponies have a good disposition, too. Besides, he's been well trained." DJ took a lead shank from a nail on the wall and snapped it to General's halter. She headed into the barn for the tack and a grooming bucket, returning moments later.

"Here." She handed her mother a brush and a rubber curry. "You want to learn how to groom him?"

"I guess." Lindy looked at the equipment in her hands. "Why do I need two?"

"You have two hands. You can work much faster and more effectively with both tools." DJ took them back and slipped her hands under the straps. "Like this." She began running the rubber curry down the pony's shoulder, followed by the brush. "You do that, and I'll get the knots out of his tail."

By the time the boys returned, the pony was groomed and tacked up.

"Maybe we should let Mom ride first." DJ looked down at the boys, whose eyes went round as silver dollars.

"Mommy knows how to ride?"

Lindy backed away, making shooing motions with her hands. "Huh-uh, not me. I wash and groom, but you guys do the riding."

DJ studied her mother. "You might like it, you know. We could put you up on a nice gentle horse. Rob—uh . . . Dad said he thinks he'd like to learn. Joe's stories of our rides up in Briones got him hooked."

Lindy continued shaking her head as she settled into the lawn chair in the shade of the barn. "Thanks anyway, but I'll watch. Every good show needs a spectator or two. Gran and I'll fill that role."

"Gran is thinking of riding." DJ kept the conversation going as she checked the girth once more. Like many horses, General had a tendency to suck in an extra breath when the saddle went on. DJ tightened the cinch another notch and led the pony over to the mounting block Robert had built for them. She motioned for Bobby to come stand beside her. She could finally tell them apart—most of the time.

"Okay, now tell me what you are going to do first."

"Put my foot in the stirrup and mount."

"You better get up on the block first, okay?" DJ held the reins in one hand, prepared to give him a boost with the other if needed. Bobby reached up to grasp the saddle, then put his foot in the stirrup and swung up like he'd been mounting horses for years rather than weeks.

"Good job." She handed him the reins. "Now get set."

The little boy was concentrating so hard that a frown deepened between his eyebrows. The helmet slipped slightly forward. He raised his chin, straightened his back, and looked to DJ. "Ready."

"Heels down." She studied his posture. "Are your reins even?"

"Uh-huh."

"Okay, walk him forward in a big circle like we did before."

After Bobby, Billy did almost as well except for his concentration. He liked looking at the scenery more.

"You are so good with them," Lindy said when they all meandered up to the house again, General now contentedly grazing back in his pasture.

"Thanks. They sure learn fast." DJ sank into one of the cushioned green iron lawn chairs now shaded by the green-and-white striped umbrella.

"You thirsty?" Maria set a tray of glasses and a pitcher of pink lemonade on the table. "Cookies in a minute. Still in oven."

"You baked cookies on a hot day like today?" Lindy leaned back against the recliner.

"Not hot in house." Maria turned back to the kitchen.

"We are so spoiled." Lindy took the moisture-beaded glass that DJ handed her.

DJ held her glass up to her cheek. "M-m-m, this feels

good. I'd thought about a shower, but since I already got wet . . ."

Lindy chuckled. "You should have seen the look on your face."

I just bet . . . DJ shook her head. *My mother never acted so goofy in her entire life—or at least the part I know*.

DJ's lesson on Herndon late that afternoon wasn't nearly as much fun as the water fight. She was learning how much she didn't know about dressage. Riding a fourth-level dressage horse was far different from learning on and training an old police horse.

"He is a powerhouse." Bridget pushed her sunglasses back up on her sweaty nose. "But just as in jumping, you have to ride him, not just sit up there like a passenger." She raised her hands. "Now, I am not saying that is what you did with Major. I am just giving advice."

DJ took in a deep breath and nodded. She did understand what Bridget was saying, but she still felt a tinge of hurt feelings. She never wanted to be "just a passenger." She signaled Herndon into a trot, and they worked shoulder-in again through the entire routine they'd done before. But this time it was right. She could tell by Bridget's smile.

DJ got home just in time for a shower before changing for dinner. Somehow, devotions after the meal seemed even more restful out on the deck with the breeze teasing the leaves above her head. She tipped her head back on the cushioned chair to listen to Robert read.

"Tonight we are going to read about a man who asked Jesus for help, and Jesus made his son well." Robert laid the Bible on his lap.

"The boy was sick, huh?" Bobby leaned on his father's shoulder.

"We're not sick," Billy offered from the other shoulder.

"No, thank God, we are all healthy." Robert traced down the page. "Now, Jesus was going all over the countryside healing people and preaching, so in this verse in John he is in Cana. 'And at Capernaum there was an official whose son was ill.' " Robert smiled at his own sons and continued to read. " 'He went and begged him to come down and heal his son, for he was at the point of death.' "

"Did the boy die?" Bobby's eyes grew round.

"Just listen, okay?" Robert continued the story until the end. " 'And he himself believed, and all his household.' "

Billy climbed in his father's lap. "I'm glad the boy didn't die. His daddy would be sad."

"His mommy, too." Now Robert had two boys in his lap. He set the Bible up on the table and wrapped his arms around them.

"So what did you learn from the story? DJ?"

"That you have to ask for help and that Jesus can heal anyone." She raised her hands. "Like He did for me on the fingernail chewing."

"And me from being sick every morning." Lindy patted her tummy.

"And me from the pneumonia." Maria crossed herself.

"Jesus made my owie all better." Bobby raised his

knee and pointed to the red spot.

"That's right. So all we have to do is ask. Who wants to pray tonight?"

Billy bounced, making his father groan. "I will. Me."

DJ closed her eyes and settled into the chair. Knowing Billy, DJ knew his prayer would be long but full of blessings. She did her own thanksgivings in her mind while Billy took care of everything else.

They'd just finished when the phone rang. Maria brought the portable to DJ.

"Young man," Maria whispered.

DJ put the receiver to her ear. "Hello?"

"Hi, this is Sean."

"Oh, hi." She could hear the lift in her voice.

"You busy?"

She shook her head, then realized he couldn't see that. "Nope, just finished dinner." She glanced up to see four pairs of eyes glued on her. She could feel the heat bloom up her neck and on her face. Trying to appear casual, she got to her feet and ambled off to the side of the deck, where she sat down on the steps, her back to her family. Giggles both childish and adult made her shake her head again.

"DJ has a boyfriend." The little-boy whisper could have been heard at the Academy.

DJ stifled the groan. *Why didn't he call on my own line?*

"I tried calling your other number, but you never answer."

Maybe I should get an answering machine for when I'm not there.

After a bit more back-and-forth, Sean said, "Are you going to the Gant thing?"

"Yep. I can't wait."

"Great. Me too. And besides, I need your professional opinion."

DJ snorted. "Yeah, like get real."

"No, you're the horse expert, not me. You know that picture I drew the day you fell off Major? I just can't get it right and thought you might help me."

"Sure, if I can. But I won't do it again just to be your model."

Sean laughed. "Would be hard, huh?"

"I've had lots of practice—I seem to take headers so much lately."

They talked for a while longer, and when she hung up, DJ realized she was alone on the deck. She leaned back against the stair post and took a deep breath. Sean was nice. *I'm glad he's going to the art school, too.* Her fingers itched to get drawing, so she ambled upstairs to her room and took out pad and pencils. As she sat down at her drawing table, DJ closed her eyes, the better to picture Stormy in some of the poses she'd thought would make good cards. Stormy was the filly Brad had given DJ after the terrible flooding in the spring.

Her pencil began to fly across the page as if it had a life of its own. Her thoughts went another direction.

DJ and her best friend, Amy, needed to spend time on their card line, but when? Summer was supposed to have all kinds of laid-back time—right? So what happened to hers?

4

ORDERS FOR MORE CARDS should have made DJ
and Amy happy.

But it didn't.

"We just have to print up more, that's all." Setting up
Thursday evening, Amy recounted the packets they had
remaining. Not enough to fill even half the orders. The
group of kids in the business club at Acalanese High
School had done more than a reasonable job. They'd
been spectacular at showing samples of the card line to
gift and card shops—and taking orders.

"So we print up as many as we have money for, de-
liver them, then print more." DJ stared at her friend.
Amy's hair was as dark as DJ's was fair, her skin tanned
a deep golden brown that could only come to someone
of Japanese descent. While DJ was tall, Amy had a
shorter frame, but they both moved with the grace of
natural athletes and loved horses almost more than people.

"Sure, that's the way we've always done it," Amy said.
"But you have to admit, that will take more time. And
cost more. I checked again, and if we could print a lot

more at a time, we could get a better price break."

"I hate this part of our card business."

Neither of them liked the bookkeeping end of their business, a card line they'd christened DJAM, Etc. DJ's pencil drawings of horses—mostly foals—and Amy's color photographs comprised the inventory.

"You know, up to now we've only sold the cards in packets, right?" DJ squinted her eyes. It helped to keep the creative thoughts coming.

"Right." Amy straightened her stack of six cards with envelopes and inserted them in the plastic bag, then taped it closed.

"What if we printed some a size larger and sold them individually? The store would still get six but not in plastic." She turned to her mother. "What do you think?"

Lindy, who sat across the picnic table assembling packets with Gran, studied the card in her hand—a fuzzy foal looking up at a bird on a branch. "I love this one and would buy it alone. You could put different messages inside. This one could say 'Where've you been? I've been looking for you.'"

"Way cool."

"Or you could flip that: 'I've been looking for you' on the outside, and 'Where've you been?' on the inside." Gran leaned back in her chair. "These are all so darling, it's no wonder people are snapping them up." Gran didn't get time with the girls very often, but since she had finished the illustrations for the last contract and hadn't signed another, they were having "ladies night." Joe, Robert, and the boys had been sent off to a movie.

Gran cocked her head. "You know, darlin', you could put a Bible verse in these and sell them to Christian bookstores, too. They have a lot of both lovely and funny cards in their stores now. I'd think any verse having to do with joy would be appropriate because joy sparkles out of these cards."

"You really think so?" DJ and Amy looked at each other and shrugged. "Why not?"

"Just who has time to call on those stores?" Amy asked no one in particular.

Now it was time for Gran and Lindy to swap *thinking* looks.

"Maybe we could." Lindy got an answering nod from her mother.

"At least right now, before the baby comes." Gran picked up another card, one of Amy's photos. "Has anyone thought to go to a service organization and offer these as a moneymaking project?"

"Huh?" DJ and Amy pulled a twins act and spoke at the same time.

"Well, I used to belong to the hospital auxiliary, and they were always looking for ways to make money to help the hospital. And a friend of mine belonged to BPW; they had the same need."

"BPW?"

"Business and Professional Women. They do all kinds of good things in the community. This way they'd be helping in two ways—assisting local young talent and earning money for their projects. Since you both are female, this might appeal to other women's groups, as well."

"You just might have something there, Mother." Lindy leaned forward, her eyes sparkling with anticipation. She turned to the girls. "If Mother or I set up an opportunity for you to meet with these groups and talk about your business, would you be willing?"

DJ and Amy both groaned.

"I'd rather scrub toilets." DJ shuddered.

"It wasn't really so bad last time." Amy half closed her eyes. "We didn't die, anyway."

"Pretty near."

"Come on, DJ, once we got going . . ."

The girls looked at each other again and shrugged. "If you get 'em, we'll go."

"And if you get any appointments for when I'm at the USET camp, Amy would love to go by herself."

"Uh-huh, and when I'm camping in the Sierras, you will."

DJ groaned again.

"What's all this groaning I hear?" Robert strolled out on the deck. "Isn't it getting a bit dark out here for heavy-duty work like you girls have been doing?"

Lindy turned and playfully smacked him on the arm. "You *girls*?"

He stepped back. "Whoa, I'm not touching that one."

"Good thing." Lindy waved him to a chair. "Where are the Bs?"

"Joe's bringing them in. They spilled their leftover popcorn in his car, and he's helping them clean it up. Or at least giving orders."

"Right." DJ knew how well Joe gave orders to his two grandsons. He was one big marshmallow where they were concerned. Unless of course they got out of hand, and then he did take care of things. She'd been on the receiving end of his *serious* face more than once.

"So I ask again, why the groans?"

"They"—DJ waved at her mother and grandmother—"want *us*"—she indicated herself and Amy—"to speak to women's groups about our business. And . . ." She paused for a moment of drama.

"Sounds like a winning idea to me. *And* what?"

"We need to print a whole bunch of cards, and we're trying to figure out how."

Robert thought a moment. "Do you accept investors?"

"What do you mean?"

"I mean, will you let me invest in your business? I will loan you the money to print your cards, and you will pay me back as the money comes in. We'll set up a contract if you like."

"Then you'll be in debt." Lindy taped another packet closed.

"But what if all of a sudden our cards quit selling?" Amy asked.

"Then your miserly banker will take the remaining money out of your hides." Robert made an evil face to match his diabolical laugh.

"I think we should stay with our old plan." Amy slapped at a mosquito.

"Time to go in. I hate bug bites." Lindy began gathering up the supplies. "We can finish this around the kitchen table."

"How much money do you need?" Robert set down the last box of cards and took a chair.

DJ and Amy both shrugged. "We haven't figured that out yet."

"I'll call and get a copy of the price breakdowns faxed over here tomorrow. Then we can talk about it again." Lindy taped her packet closed.

"Seems to me you girls are on the brink of needing to make some decisions, like whether to grow larger or stay where you are. And like your mother suggested a few weeks ago, T-shirts would be a great sideline, and maybe a book or two." Robert began picking up the cards in the proper order to package.

"A book?" DJ looked at Amy, and they both shook their heads.

"We just needed money to support our horse habit. Don't you think this is getting out of hand?" DJ propped her elbows on the table and stared down at the foal sniffing a butterfly on a flower. What she really wanted to do was go see Stormy again. One week out of the summer wasn't nearly enough, and here it was almost time to leave for the USET jumping camp.

"We picked up all the popcorn. Now the birds can eat it." The boys handed their sacks to their father. "Daddy, can we use the dust sucker?"

DJ hid a giggle behind her hand. She knew they meant Dustbuster, the handheld vacuum that hung on the wall in the garage.

"Sure. I'll get it down." Robert got to his feet and left with a boy on each hand.

Joe leaned against the counter. "Is there any of that ice cream left?"

Gran's eyebrows danced up and down. "What happened to your diet?"

Joe groaned.

DJ pushed her chair back. "I'll dish it up. Thanks, GJ."

That night in her prayers, DJ brought up the matter of the card business. "God, I don't know what you want me—us—to do here. Mom and Dad have such good ideas, but they all cost so much. I know they would help with the money, but . . ." She paused and studied the shadow patterns on her wall. "I don't know, it all just seems too much at times. I just want to draw, not all that other stuff." She fought against her eyelids drifting closed. Once that happened, she'd be asleep immediately. "Thank you for helping me not chew my fingernails. Now, about this fear thing. You know, it's hard to pray for something that isn't happening. At least I can't tell any differences. Maybe I should start lighting matches and see if that helps." The thought made her stomach clench. "Okay, so what do I do?" She waited, wishing for an answer. All she could feel was *Wait*. Was that an answer? "So here it is. Thank you for taking away my fear of fire. Thank you for my business with Amy, thank you for Herndon, and mostly thank you that Major is better. I can see what you did there. Amen."

She turned over and read again the verse she'd chosen to memorize. *"Truly, truly, I say to you, if you ask anything of the Father, he will give it to you in my name. Hitherto you have asked nothing in my name; ask, and you will receive, that your joy may be full."* She read it three times and then repeated it from memory, stumbling a little.

They left for the show on Friday as soon as Hilary got home from summer school. They wanted to get to Sacramento before the traffic got bad. DJ rode with Joe, who pulled the four-horse trailer, while Hilary and Tony rode with Bunny in her new motor home.

"You could have ridden with the others if you'd wanted." Joe tipped his head back toward the vehicle following them. They'd been on the road about an hour.

"No, I'm perfectly happy here."

"You could have stretched out on the bed there, more comfortable to sleep."

DJ stretched and let her left arm fall to pat her grandfather's shoulder. "Sorry, I didn't plan on sleeping like that."

"Have you noticed lately that whenever you get in a car, it's not long before you're asleep?"

DJ shook her head. "Nope, hadn't thought about it." She stared out the windshield. She had been tired lately—for a long time, if she was honest. "There's just too much I want to do, I guess. Sleeping isn't one of my top priorities."

Joe glanced at her and shook his head. "Getting enough sleep is important for a growing girl."

"Huh. I've been this tall for two years now. I think I quit growing." She lifted one bare foot, leaving her sandal on the truck floor. "Except for my feet. I need new boots again. Mine are too tight."

"There will probably be a good selection in the vendor booths under the grandstand at the showgrounds."

"I didn't bring *that* kind of money with me."

"I did."

"Joe, you can't keep buying me things. I have money in my savings account."

"Why can't I?"

"Because." She didn't want to say that her mother got tight-lipped when others spent large sums of money for her daughter.

"Just consider them part of my investment."

DJ groaned. Somehow she would keep him away from the boot booth. She would stay away, as well.

"That's why I hate to tell you some things. You and Robert and Brad."

"Darla Jean Randall, do you ever ask me for anything?"

She thought a moment. "Sure, for rides from school, taking care of my horse in the morning, coming to shows with me like today, all kinds of stuff."

Joe shook his head. "That's not what I meant. *Things*, like stuff. Like boots or a CD or a book or—"

"You could buy me an ice-cream cone." DJ giggled at the look on her grandfather's face. "Okay, a milk shake, then."

She laughed out loud when he pulled off the freeway at the next exit and into a strip mall that housed an ice-cream store. By the time he'd bought milk shakes all around and they were back on the road, DJ was still laughing. She alternately sucked on the straw and shook her head.

"See!" She hoisted her milk shake container. "That's just why I try not to say anything." She giggled again. "Besides, did you see the surprised look on Bunny's face when we stopped?"

"Well, if you don't like yours, I'll finish it." Joe set his drink back in the cup holder. "Man, that hits the spot. Good idea, kid."

Later, when they could finally unload the horses at the show barns, Herndon walked to his stall as if he were king and everyone ought to bow. He nickered and then whinnied at the responses.

"You big show-off," DJ said, a firm hand on the lead shank. "Knock it off." She jerked gently when he whinnied right in her ear. She watched the numbers of the stalls and led him into the one that corresponded with her entry pass. She swung the door shut behind them before removing the lead shank so he could explore the box stall. As he sniffed in the corners, she checked the depth of the sawdust and looked for any nails sticking out from the walls.

Bunny took the stall on DJ's right, Hilary on the left. Next to Hilary was Tony, and then their tack room, which they would have to decorate. As soon as the horses were fed and watered, the four riders started moving in the tack boxes. They hung the sign and the royal blue draping, then hooked the brass-toned name-plates on the doors and swept the floor of the tack room.

"There, that looks good." Hilary dusted off her hands. "Now we can exercise the horses before everyone else is here and needs the arenas, too."

By the time they'd ridden, visited with riders they'd met at other shows, and eaten dinner, night had fallen. The tempo at the grounds didn't abate, however, as the line of rigs entering the gates stretched down the road. This A-rated show had a top reputation; therefore, the classes would be large and running in three rings from 8:00 in the morning until 8:00 or later at night, then start the same on Sunday and run until it was finished.

"Okay, you all have your things ready for in the morning?" Bunny looked to each of her teammates and waited for their nods. "Good. Then let's get out the soda and chips. I brought UNO to play this time."

DJ looked around the teal and gray interior of the new motor home. Everything matched, from the furniture to the curtains and carpets. Like the girls were really roughing it to stay in an outfit like this one. DJ caught Joe's glance and rolled her eyes.

He grinned back and began shuffling the cards.

Talk got around to what the kids wanted to do with their lives. Hilary laid a card on the pile before answering Bunny. "I'm taking pre-law. Finally declared my major last week. I wasn't sure if I wanted a business degree or not, but I realized I want to help make things better for people. Law is one way to do that."

"That's a hard major when you spend so much time on the road with your horses."

"I know, but . . ." Hilary smiled at Tony and DJ. "We three are going to be on the Olympic team someday, and if it takes me longer to get through college and law school, that's just the way it is."

"What about you, Tony?" Joe gathered in the hand after playing his last card.

"No fair," Tony grumbled. "I hate playing games with you. You always win."

"You'll be a senior this year, right?"

"M-hmm. I told my dad I'd like to be a rich playboy, and he said I'd have to find someone else to support my life-style—he couldn't, and wouldn't, afford it." Tony shook his head. "Sheesh, like I was asking for the moon or something." His grin said he was teasing.

"So what did you decide to do?"

"Marry rich."

Hilary socked him on the shoulder. "That's supposed to be a girl's line, you nut."

"Well, s-o-r-r-y. We can't all be like DJ. Already a successful businesswoman, and she's only fourteen."

"Almost fifteen." DJ played her card.

"And she already knows what she wants to do." Bunny slapped her card on the table. "If I were that kind of artist, I'd go for it, too. I get more compliments on that drawing you did of Felix. I have it hanging over the mantel in the living room."

DJ felt the heat begin to color her neck.

After two more hands, Joe declared himself the winner. "Time for lights-out. I'll call you all at 5:00, right? Come on, Tony."

DJ groaned along with the rest. No wonder she was tired all the time.

Saturday afternoon Herndon acted like all the applause was just for him. But he'd really earned it this time. Two blue ribbons and a rosette for Equitation in their flatwork. When they took only a second in Hunter on the Flat, the people in the audience made their displeasure known.

"You and that horse sure look mighty pretty out there, little lady," one of the spectators said when she exited the arena.

"Thank you." DJ stroked Herndon's sweaty neck. *Now, if we can work together like this over the jumps tomorrow.*

They were first out on Sunday morning. DJ caught sight of Bridget, who couldn't come until today, sitting with Bunny and Hilary in the stands just when they called her number.

"Okay, big guy, let's just forget everything and give it our best." DJ signaled him to a trot and pointed him at the first jump, a simple post and rail. *"Keep him between your hands and legs, ride aggressively, look to the center base of the next jump."* DJ could hear Bridget's voice in her head. Straight on. *Three, two, one,* and they were flying. Her heart soared like Herndon's body. They landed perfectly, and with Herndon's ears pricked forward, they cantered toward the oxer. Around to the in and out, straight on to the brush, each time sailing like they'd never had a hesitation or doubt in their lives. At the last fence, a triple, Herndon landed, then flicked his tail and gave a grunt.

DJ wanted to stand in her stirrups and shout to the heavens like Pat Day did when he won the Kentucky Derby. But she kept her cool and her seat and trotted out of the arena.

Thank you, God. Thank you, thank you, thank you.

"That was magnificent." Joe smiled up at her.

"Now, if we can only do it again."

5

THAT'S OUR NUMBER.

Joe patted DJ's knee. "You can do it, darlin', you can do it."

"Th-thanks." Though the endearment was Gran's, even coming in a male voice, it comforted DJ. She sucked in a deep breath, let it all out, repeated the action, and signaled Herndon into a trot. To anyone watching, DJ appeared totally in control, professional far beyond her years. All she could think was a wish for her butterflies to give it a rest.

The jumps had been raised four inches. Herndon flicked his tail and pointed his ears. They led into a canter, straight for the first jump. As they cleared it with a foot or more to spare, DJ could feel her cheeks crease in a wide grin. Her horse was having just as much fun as she was—and they were a team.

The chicken coop looked larger but not enough to slow them down. "Easy, fella," she sang to his twitching ears. Herndon responded by releasing even more power, and they sailed over the jump. DJ wanted to scream and shout, but she kept her focus right where it belonged—

at the center base of the next jump.

Too soon they were done and cantering out the gate. The applause broke out, ebbed, then swelled again.

Were those tears in Joe's eyes or just watering brought on by the dust?

"That was prettier than any picture I've ever seen." The big man took hold of Herndon's reins and pounded on his neck. He grinned up at DJ, shaking his head. "Man, that was pure symphony."

DJ patted Herndon's neck, wanting more to throw her arms around it and squeeze. "What a round! Joe, I've never felt quite like that before—like we could jump the moon if someone would harness it for us." She thumped on Herndon's shoulder. "Way to go, horse, way to go."

"When you get something right, you go all the way." Joe squeezed her hand. "And to think your dads missed this. What a shame."

"There'll be more. I can tell." She shifted in the saddle. "How about holding him while I run for the rest room? All that soda . . ." DJ dismounted as she asked.

"Sure, but you better hustle."

"I will."

There was still one more jumper to finish the round when DJ returned to the practice ring.

Tony rode up beside her. "So we go again."

"I know. You two looked great out there."

"Thanks, but you are stealing the show. That horse loves to jump. You can see it in every muscle."

"Thank you." DJ took Herndon by the cheek straps of the bridle and looked him straight on. "You are one awesome horse, you know that?"

Herndon snorted and raised his head to snuffle her cheek. DJ felt the tingling clear down to her toes. "That tickles." She patted him once more and mounted. Herndon had actually acted as though he cared about her. Maybe they were getting to be friends after all. And Tony was right; the big gelding loved to jump. He was a show-off from the nails in his shoes to the tips of his ears, including his long eyelashes. She thought again of Tony's comments. Sure was a big change from when he first came to the Academy. From redneck to nice guy. Wow!

"Thanks, GJ. I sure do feel better." DJ trotted Herndon around the practice ring, along with the three other contestants who'd jumped perfect rounds.

"Way to go, you two." Hilary leaned on the fence rail, Bunny beside her.

Bridget nodded, her eyes sparkling. "I told you so."

DJ waved and kept Herndon to an even pace.

"All right, folks, we're about ready for the next round of jumping. Number forty-three, DJ Randall on Herndon, will be jumping first."

DJ patted Herndon's neck one last time and signaled a walk over to the closed gate that led into the arena.

The steward at the ingate smiled up at her. "It'll be just a minute or two if you want to go around again."

"Thanks." DJ reined Herndon to the side and kept him moving. When the gate swung open, she turned back and trotted through. Applause greeted them, but DJ only had eyes and ears for the first jump. Up four more inches. Now it was beginning to show. *Please, God.*

She signaled a canter, and like an arrow heading for a target, they approached the first jump. *Three, two, one . . .* DJ could feel her horse gather himself and catapult them into the air. Controlled, rounded, focused. She could have picked a star from the sky like an apple from a tree. After a smooth landing, she looked to the next jump when he lifted off. Her hands followed up his neck as she arched over his withers.

DJ looked around the corner to the next jump, and Herndon landed on the right lead. "Easy," she murmured as he picked up speed. At the triple, they seemed to hang in the air forever but touched ground in perfect time and on to the next.

No tick marred the perfection of the round, and the applause let her know that the audience appreciated their efforts.

DJ could hardly think for the wonder of it. All her life she'd wanted to jump, and here she was with an incredible horse and the jumps flowing beneath them like water under a bridge. And like the bridge, her horse held power beyond her understanding.

DJ dashed the moisture from her eyes before she got to Joe, who waited off to the side. Her butterflies did cartwheels, but now she didn't care. They were doing them all in formation like a well-trained ballet troupe.

"You want something to drink?" Joe clamped a hand on her knee.

"Water."

"Here." Bunny handed over a bottle.

"Thanks." DJ chugged it, letting some dribble down her chin. Up until now, she hadn't realized it was getting hot out. She wiped her forehead and listened for the next number. Tony trotted up to her.

"That was some ride."

"Thanks." She patted Herndon's shoulder again. "He's having a good time."

"That's obvious."

Just then they heard a crack and the sound of a falling bar. The groan from the spectators told what had happened. While the rider finished the round, he was now out of the running since DJ had jumped a perfect round.

"Good luck," she called as Tony trotted toward the gate.

He waved back at her and entered the arena when his number was called.

The least I can get is third place. DJ turned Herndon so she could watch Tony jump. Like her and Herndon, they looked to be having a good time. As he launched over the jump, the tick sounded loud, but the groan from the stands turned to relief when the bar only wobbled and stayed in place. Tony made a brow-sopping motion as he came out of the arena.

DJ laughed when he trotted up to her and rolled his eyes. "Close, huh?"

"Yeah, I dropped him." Tony patted his horse's shoulder. "Sorry, big guy. That was my fault. I won't do it again."

They both trotted around the ring while waiting for the last entrant to complete her round. A bar falling on the final jump knocked her out, too.

Tony and DJ grinned at each other. "Well, it's you and me," he said. "Someday we're going to be like this at the Olympics. The final jump-off."

"So we just do our best. Good luck."

"And to you." Tony cocked his head. "Loser buys lunch?"

"Get your money out." DJ nudged Herndon to a trot, and they completed another circuit of the practice ring.

"Heavenly Father, thanks for the ride so far, and please help us continue to do our best."

Trotting into the ring, DJ looked across the jumps.

She'd never jumped that high before, in competition or practice. She trotted Herndon in a circle and signaled a canter as they headed for the first jump. *Three, two, one.* Like shot from a catapult, they left the ground and soared through the air.

DJ forgot the height of the jumps. She forgot everything but the next obstacle. Each time Herndon launched himself in the air, she cheered within. When they cleared the stone wall, it was like she woke from a trance—she'd been so focused on what they were doing that nothing else existed.

The audience clapped and cheered, and once she'd cleared the gate, DJ let herself hear them.

"Wave." Joe stood beside her. DJ did as he told her, all the while shaking her head.

"I can't believe we did that. Joe, those jumps looked big enough to . . . to . . . ." She couldn't think of the words. "What if we have to go again?"

The applause told her that Tony had entered the ring. She was almost afraid to look.

On one hand, she didn't want him to knock a bar down, but on the other . . . the thought of jumping even higher sent DJ's butterflies into a frenzy.

She could hear Tony's horse grunt with the effort. "Go, Tony, you can do it!" They ticked on the oxer, but the bar stayed in place. She groaned with the other spectators and breathed a sigh of relief when they cleared the next jump.

"Come on." Joe gripped her knee, his eyes on the ring.

She'd almost let out the breath she didn't realize she'd been holding, when the crack made her sigh. Down went the bar, and Tony cantered out of the ring.

"And our winner is DJ Randall on Herndon."

DJ patted Herndon's sweaty neck and trotted back into the arena. Her first blue ribbon in jumping at a big-time show like this. She accepted the blue rosette with a smile fit to split her face.

"Congratulations, young lady. That was some fine jumping."

"Thank you." Waving the rosette, they trotted back out. She grinned at Tony as he met her going in. "You owe me."

"I know. Congratulations." His horse swirled his tail as Tony ordered a canter.

Coming in near the top wasn't as exciting for Tony as it was for DJ. He'd been there before—many times. DJ handed Joe the ribbon and, leaning forward, draped her arms around Herndon's neck. "Horse, we did it."

"You sure did, and with class to spare. You could have gone another round just fine."

"I'm glad we didn't have to. That brush jump looked like a monster to me, but Herndon never hesitated." DJ straightened up and looked down at her grandfather. "I never dreamed it could feel like that. Talk about power." She patted Herndon's sweaty neck. "Oh man."

Bunny, Bridget, and Hilary clustered around when Tony joined them. "You two were awesome."

"Except DJ's more awesome than me." Tony put the red ribbon against the black of his coat. "Looks good, huh?"

"Hers is better." Hilary grinned up at DJ. "Ya done good, buddy."

"I still can't believe we did it." DJ shook her head. "That was the most awesome—I mean, I thought the round before was incredible, but this . . . Those jumps looked like giant trees."

"And they get bigger. And it's timed when you move up to the next division." Bunny shook her head. "When the jump is taller than I am, I begin to panic."

DJ smiled down at her petite friend. "Of course, being bigger than you isn't hard."

"Hush your mouth, young pup." Bunny nudged DJ with her shoulder.

"Now you know how the big jumps feel," Bridget said with a smile. "And you loved it. That is good." She patted Herndon's neck. "You two make a good team."

DJ accepted the congratulations of people walking by, all the while stroking Herndon's neck. The big horse beside her took the extra pats and compliments as if he played the celebrity every day. Joe stood on his other side, like DJ, one hand on Herndon's bridle. When two girls who looked to be about ten stopped to admire Herndon, he snuffled one girl's hand and bobbed his head.

"Look at him." DJ nodded at her horse. From high-flier to back to earth, there was none of the snobbishness she'd felt in him before. Could a horse understand honors and a job well done?

"I have something for you," Joe said on the way home. He reached for a package behind the seat and handed the bag to her.

"What?" DJ felt the hard sides.

"Open it, for pete's sake."

DJ let out a whoosh of air when she pulled out a

video. She looked at him with shining eyes. "My jumping?"

"Yours and the others—your whole class. That way
you can see what the others did wrong, too."

"Ah, Joe, you are the best." She unbuckled her seat
belt so she could kiss his cheek. "You are so good to me."

"DJ, darlin', you are easy to be good to." He cleared
his throat and sniffed, as did she.

Telling her family about it that night was almost as
good as doing it over.

"Sure wish we had been there." Lindy looked up at
Robert, who was standing right behind her with his
hands on her shoulders. "Next time we plan the company picnic around the horse shows."

"Then we better have it in January." Robert smiled at
DJ. "Sure hope you got good pictures."

DJ shrugged. "Amy wasn't there, so I don't know. I
think Bunny had a camera along. I can ask for the one
they took on presentation. That'll be something." She
leaned over and mischievously pulled a flat package out
from beside the cushion. "Of course, Joe did get this for
me." She waved the video in the air. "I just thought you
might like to see it, but it can wait for another time if
you want."

"If we want?" Robert grabbed the video and crossed
the room to insert it in the VCR. By the time it finished
running, the boys were cheering, and DJ again felt the
ecstasy of the moment.

Robert and Lindy stared at her, shaking their heads.
"And to think you are our daughter," Robert said.

"Thank you, heavenly Father," Lindy whispered. She
wrapped an arm around her daughter and hugged her
close. "You were magnificent."

With the video tape to review, DJ hoped she could keep the picture and feeling fresh in her mind. She'd do replays like Bridget talked about. Replay what she did right and preplay doing it right again. Now she had a *real* event to replay and preplay. They'd done it right, that was for sure.

"Maybe if there's a good shot of you jumping, you could do it over in pencil and we could frame it like the one of Stormy. That would be a real treasure." Robert sat down between DJ and her mother and put an arm around each of them, drawing them close to his sides. "Of course, we could always take it off the video if we need to. Might get the best one that way." The twins had calmed down again and now lay on the floor watching a *Veggie Tales* video. Their feet waved in the air in time with the excitement of the video.

DJ almost called them to join the rest on the sofa. What a cool family she had.

"I better go call Brad. They'll want to know about this, too." She kissed Robert on the cheek and slid to her feet. "Don't go away. I'll be back."

The next morning at 7:00, Robert dropped DJ off at the Pleasant Hill BART—Bay Area Rapid Transit—station so she could take the train into San Francisco.

"You know what bus to catch now, right?"

DJ stopped in the act of opening the truck door. "I do, and where to get off and how to get back to BART and—"

"Okay, okay, I get the point. But you can't blame me for being a bit protective. I never had a daughter before, especially one old enough to get around San Francisco on her own."

DJ didn't tell him about the butterflies that were going at their stir-up-her-insides act. Granted, she and Gran had taken the route one day in June, but things could still go wrong. "You told me I had to learn to trust God to take care of me, remember?"

Robert grimaced. "Hung by my own tongue, right?"

"Huh?" Her eyebrows pulled her eyes wide open.

"Nothing. See you this evening. Call when you—"

"Get back here to the station, I know." DJ blew him a kiss and, tucking her drawing case under her arm, slammed the truck door behind her. She dug the twenty-dollar bill out of her pocket and inserted it in the slot on the front of the silver-toned ticket machine. After she punched the ticket button, her ticket clicked its way out another slot. Taking the white card stock ticket that would last most of the week, she walked across to the turnstiles, stuck her ticket in the arrowed slot, and when the ticket popped up, walked through the turnstile. She was on her way.

She'd brought a book to read on the train but found watching people more interesting as more commuters filled the car with each stop. Herndon had earned the day off, that was for sure, and Joe promised to take care of him every morning just like during school. Truth was, she'd been going to school every morning all summer. But such fun schooling. First Diablo Valley College, and now the San Francisco School of Art.

DJ thought of the pots she would pick up after the final firing. If the one for her mother turned out like she hoped, she'd be really pleased. Mr. Charles had talked about her taking another class, but that wouldn't be until next summer. Instead, she now had a week of drawing with renowned artist Isabella Gant.

The little bounce she gave on the seat drew the gaze of the woman beside her. DJ settled back in her seat. Strange how the ride seemed so much longer when she was by herself.

DJ exited from the BART train at the Montgomery Street exit like she and Gran had practiced so she could catch her bus. After riding up the long escalator, she followed the commuter crowd out into the courtyard and then up the stairs to Montgomery. Waiting in the sun, DJ glanced across Market Street at the Sheraton Palace Hotel, where she and Gran had gone for tea in the Garden Court room. She remembered how the arched ceiling made of millions of panes of glass and crystal had taken her breath away and how the music flowing from the harp had brought it back. One of these days, maybe they could go back there—and she'd take a sketch pad.

The sound of a cat crying made her look down and behind her. There sat a mound of rags, the woman inside them looking older and more worn than the antique streetlamps that lined the curb. A stocking cap that was more holes than cap covered stringy gray hair and half covered one eye. The black-and-white cat on a leash and harness arched its back and rubbed against DJ's leg. A brisk wind funneled down the skyscraper canyon and made DJ glad she'd worn jeans and a Windbreaker. One could always pick out tourists in San Francisco during the summer because they froze to death in their shorts and tank tops.

"He likes you." The mound moved, and the woman's smile showed missing teeth.

"Can I pet him?" DJ knew her mother would have a

fit, but then, her mother wasn't here.

"Sure, dearie." The woman cuddled a younger, half-grown yellow cat under her chin. "He never can get enough loves."

DJ bent down and stroked the black-and-white cat's back. He looked up at her. His Charlie Chaplin mustache, one white ear, and one black ear gave him a quizzical look. "Most cats aren't this friendly."

"I know." The woman chuckled and bobbed her head again. "That's why he's my best friend. Calls him Charlie, I do."

A bus pulled up, and DJ straightened to see if it was hers. She bent down to pat the cat again when it wasn't. *I wonder if she's had anything to eat today. The cats look better off than she does*. Charlie sat and, tail twitching at the tip, batted at DJ's leg.

Another bus arrived. This time it was hers.

DJ dug in her pocket and pulled out a dollar. She patted the cat once more and handed the money to the lady. "Here, I hope this helps." *What a stupid thing to say*.

"Why, thankee, dearie. That's right good of you." The woman, her hands covered by gloves with no fingers, took the dollar and tucked it into her coat. "You have a nice day now, hear?"

"I will." After pushing her way onto the bus, DJ bent over to look out the window where the street woman now had Charlie cuddled up against her, a cat in each arm. *I wish I'd given her all my lunch money. Maybe if she's there tomorrow* . . .

Thoughts of the homeless woman plagued her all the way to her bus stop. Her fingers tingled, a sure sign they wanted to draw the homeless woman. She'd been so friendly, not at all like the homeless people portrayed in stories DJ had heard. *Where does she get food for her cats? I wish I'd brought a camera.*

When the bus reached her stop, DJ stood and walked to the door.

"Hi, DJ." Sean stepped up to greet her when she got off the bus.

"How'd you know when I'd get here?" A familiar face looked even better than usual right about then.

"Just figured it out." He swung into step beside her. "How was the show this weekend?"

DJ spent the entire walk to the art room telling him about the horse show.

"I go to sleep remembering that incredible feeling of . . . of power and control and . . ." She paused and closed her eyes for just a second. "And flying. I've always wondered what the astronauts feel like in space with no gravity, and I think jumping is about the closest I'll ever come. Sean, you've got to try it sometime."

"I'd have to learn to ride first." He shifted his portfolio from one arm to the other. "Let's get seats and I'll show you my drawing. Horses aren't the easiest to draw, you know. And someone taking a header off one isn't easy, either."

DJ groaned. "I bet." But she studied the picture when Sean flipped it open. "Part of the problem is you have Major's neck too short." She shook her head. "Boy, that's a great one of me. I thought you were my friend."

"I am. But this I couldn't resist. So, okay, if I lengthen his neck, what else?"

DJ studied the drawing some more. "His legs aren't quite right." She closed her eyes to think how a halting horse would look. "See, put him back more on his haunches and his head up more. I hate eating dirt, and that's what happened next. Felt like an idiot."

"Thanks." Sean flipped the pages back in place as two friends from the spring session joined them at the high table. They caught up on all their news while the others trickled in.

By the time the classroom was full, there were people of all ages. *Gran could have come.* DJ looked around and returned several smiles. She hooked her feet over the rungs of the stool and faced forward when Ms. Gant blew into the room. Like the twins, she was energy in perpetual motion, her long, more pepper than salt hair woven into a knot near the top of her head and anchored with what looked like two black chopsticks. She was dressed in black straight-legged pants and a black turtleneck. The shawl she wore held every shade of purple and pink, its threads of silver shimmering with her every move. As usual, her necklace of stones and beads and coins made DJ's fingers itch to sketch it.

How would she capture the energy that swirled about and through Isabella Gant? DJ studied her teacher through slitted eyes. The eyes, that's what it was—the eyes needed to be the central focus.

After greeting the class and calling the roll, Ms. Gant flung her shawl over the back of her chair and whipped the cover off a still life. "We will start with this. I want to see what you do before I tell you what I want you to do."

DJ and Sean exchanged glances. They'd heard that before.

DJ laid out her pencils and flipped open her drawing pad. Did she dare cheat and draw the teacher instead?

6

"AH, SO YOU KNOW BETTER than the teacher?"

DJ froze. "N-n-no. I just . . . ah . . ." The drawing had happened almost of its own volition. "I . . . I . . . ah, thought to hurry with this one and then do the still life." The words came in a rush.

"I see."

DJ felt like crawling under the stool, but instead she chose to freeze like a bunny caught in a flashlight beam. She wanted to keep drawing. She wanted to look at her teacher. Her fingers shivered and DJ dropped the drawing pencil. The lead broke.

"I think the hair is not quite right yet, a bit out of proportion to the face and body." Ms. Gant tapped the drawing pad as she spoke. "And what did you plan to do with the shawl?"

"Lace in bits of pink and purple, and catch the light with silver." DJ studied her drawing through squinted eyes. "The eyes aren't right yet, either." She looked at the woman who stood beside her, wishing she dared ask her to return to the front of the room and hold a pose like one of the models she'd brought in last spring.

"But this was to be done in pencil."

"I know. But you asked what I would do, and I would do the shawl first in pencil and then add the color. It needs that bit of color to be what I see."

"Ah." Her eyebrows winged higher. "There are many things wrong with it, but as usual, you have caught the spirit. I have been called a 'first cousin to a whirling dervish,' and you have captured at least a hint of that kind of energy." She walked around DJ and studied the drawing from another angle. "I did say to do as you like first, didn't I?"

DJ half shrugged. "Sort of." She wanted to ask, "When holding a drawing pencil, do your fingers have a mind of their own?" But she didn't have the courage. After all, she *was* supposed to be drawing a still life, not the teacher.

"You will fix this?"

"If it's all right."

"It will be better than all right when you are finished." Ms. Gant whirled on to the next student, leaving DJ gasping for air.

That night at home, DJ told her mother about the class, but she didn't mention the homeless woman and her cats. "You should see the picture Sean drew of me taking a header off Major at the show." DJ shook her head. "I can still taste the dirt."

Lindy shuddered. "Don't remind me." She flipped the drawing pad to the picture of Ms. Gant. "Darla Jean, this is really good."

DJ cocked her head and studied the drawing. "I still

don't have her eyes just right. She's hard to draw 'cause she's never still. Not for a minute." She almost mentioned the homeless woman and how she wanted to draw her, but she stopped herself. She knew her mother would tell her not to stop again, but DJ couldn't get the woman and the cats out of her mind.

The next morning DJ started pulling things from the refrigerator.

"What you doing?" Maria asked.

"Making a sandwich."

"For lunch?"

"Umm." *But not for me.* DJ made two sandwiches, bagged some peanut butter cookies, and added a bag of chips. After thinking for a minute, she got out the block of cheese and cut two chunks, one for herself and one for the lady. The bag was pretty full by the time she put in two juices, but when Maria cocked a questioning eyebrow, DJ just shrugged.

"Ah, you make lunch for that nice boy, too, eh?"

DJ could feel the heat surge up her face. "Maria!"

"He nice on phone." She pointed to the table. "You sit, I bring breakfast."

DJ sat. Robert tipped his paper down enough to wink at her.

She probably won't be there, DJ thought as she followed the crowd up the stairs at Montgomery. *Then Sean and I really will have a picnic. Not that he'd understand*

the dog kibbles I put in for the cats.

Charlie greeted her like an old friend. DJ leaned down to pet him, then smiled at the woman. "Is it okay if I brought you something?" There, she'd gotten it out. What if the lady was offended? DJ handed her the sack of food and the plastic bag of kibbles. "I . . . I just thought maybe you . . . you . . ." It wasn't the wind that made her cheeks hot, she knew that.

"Ah, dearie." The woman opened the sack and after studying the contents looked up at DJ. "You be one good person, little girl. Me and my cats, we thank you." The woman opened the plastic bag and poured a bit of the dried food into an empty tuna can for the cats to share.

DJ squatted down and ran her hand over Charlie's back while he ate. The bus pulled up and DJ stood. "See you tomorrow." Backpack flopping with the lighter weight, she joined the throng all trying to get on the bus at the same time. She looked out the window in time to see the woman giving one of her sandwiches to a man who looked to be in the same shape as she. DJ resolved to bring more in the morning.

Once at school, the morning's drawing wouldn't come together. The male model, dressed in jeans and a cotton shirt with rolled-back sleeves, sat with his head on his chest as if he were sleeping. But all DJ could see was the woman with her cats. She flipped her paper to the next sheet and started again.

"You are having a problem?" Ms. Gant stopped at DJ's side.

"Umm." DJ sighed. "All I keep seeing is this woman who sits by where I get on the bus. She has two cats and lives on the streets, I think."

"So . . ." The teacher paused and traced a line with

her finger. "What if you draw the woman, get her out of your head, and then draw our model?"

"Could I?" DJ flipped the page and grinned at her teacher. "You are the best."

"Thank you." Ms. Gant patted DJ's shoulder as she went on to talk with Sean.

But the woman wouldn't come right, either. DJ wished she could take her pad down to Montgomery and Market and sketch right there. After several attempts, though, she felt free of the idea and went back to working on the model. Horses were always easier than people.

The entire week went that way. DJ felt off kilter, as if she was either a step ahead or a step behind the others. She often had lunch with Sean and another girl, and they said much the same thing. Life with Isabella Gant was anything but boring.

DJ sketched Sean eating an apple. She added bits of color to a still life that was to be done in black-and-white, but that was after Ms. Gant had deemed the drawing finished. A weeping cherry tree appeared on her pad as if by magic.

She had no time to worry about the USET camp. Right now she lived in a world of pencils, paper, erasers, and line. Fat lines, skinny lines, wiggly lines—they grew and shifted and formed new life on her drawing pad.

The thrill was like the thrill she felt when jumping—only not nearly as intense. More like taking low fences in perfect form.

On Wednesday DJ brought more food and a blanket

she'd stuffed in her backpack. She'd ignored Maria's questioning looks but told Robert what she was doing on their way to the BART station.

"Darla Jean Randall, you are one amazing kid." Robert leaned over and kissed her on the cheek. "And happy fifteenth birthday, daughter." He dug in his pocket and handed her a five-dollar bill. "Stick this in that sack you give her."

"Thanks." DJ scrambled from the pickup. "You're the greatest."

After giving over her stash to the woman, DJ asked, "What's your name?"

"Emma." The woman grinned up at DJ. "Round here they call me Emma Two Cats." Her chortle made a few heads turn. "You be one good person, dearie. Can't never say thank you enough."

The bus arrived with a *whoosh* of brakes.

"See ya."

Later that morning, Ms. Gant stood in front of class and said to DJ, "I would like to see your new note cards. Would you bring them in?"

"I . . . I guess, if you want."

"I want. And now Sean has something to say." She beckoned Sean to come forward.

He smiled at DJ as he stood beside Ms. Gant. "Today is a special day for someone in this class. DJ Randall turns fifteen."

DJ's face flamed hotter than a second-degree sunburn when Ms. Gant began singing. At the end, she stuttered over the thank-you, but in spite of the heat, she knew her face would crack from her wide smile any minute.

Sean turned around and fished a wrapped package

from under the desk. "Since DJ helped me with this, by both being the model and adjusting some lines, I probably shouldn't give this as a birthday present, but I am anyway." He walked over to DJ's stool and handed her the flat box.

"Th-thank you." DJ knew what it was. His drawing of her taking a header off Major. She unwrapped and opened the box with everyone watching her.

Sure enough. But with Sean's finishing touches and in a beautiful frame, the picture had turned out better than DJ remembered. She shook her head. "Couldn't you do one of me going *over* the jump with the horse?" She held it up so everyone could see. "Thanks, Sean."

Sean smiled and returned to his stool. "How did you know it was my birthday?" DJ whispered.

"I asked your mother," he whispered back. "And I also asked her if I could take you out to dinner after class."

"You're kidding."

He shook his head. "Wait and see."

That evening after a bus ride to Columbus Street, Sean took DJ's hand as they walked down the street. DJ bumped him with her shoulder. "What are ya doin'?"

Sean shrugged. "I don't want anyone to get between us, okay?"

DJ shrugged. "Okay." Besides, it felt kind of nice, better than keeping her hands in her pockets now that the cool fog had drifted back through the streets of the city.

"But I'm not dressed up for a restaurant like that," DJ said when they stopped in front of the Stinking Rose.

"No matter. Other people aren't dressed up, either. Come on, I have reservations."

DJ followed him inside and past the line of patrons waiting for admittance. She'd never been out to dinner with a guy before. Did everyone in the line know it? The white-aproned waiter led them clear through the restaurant permeated by the smell of garlic. Dried garlic ropes garlanded the walls, along with pictures of garlic, garlic recipes, and huge jars filled with pickled garlic cloves. DJ was so busy looking around and still trying to keep up with Sean that she stopped short at a loud shout of "Surprise!"

There in front of DJ sat Lindy, Robert, and the boys, Gran and Joe, Brad and Jackie, and Amy. DJ was surprised, all right.

"What . . . who. . . ?" DJ couldn't get the words out. She glanced at Sean, who just shrugged and grinned.

"Sit down, birthday girl," Joe said. "Have some garlic bread."

By the time they'd all eaten their fill of garlic chicken, garlic bread, and garlic mashed potatoes, DJ could only shake her head when Joe asked if she wanted garlic ice cream. When the birthday cake arrived, there were no candles, but the number 15 was written in bright icing.

DJ smiled her thanks to her mother and Gran and after cutting the cake gave the twins the first pieces. Surely there wouldn't be garlic in the frosting?

"Open your presents," Bobby or Billy—she wasn't sure at the moment—commanded.

DJ eyed the stack the waiter had set up on another table. She shook her head and glanced around at her entire family. "You guys."

"Hurry," the other twin added.

"Okay, you bring them to me."

Both boys bailed out of their seats and each grabbed at the same package from the bottom of the pile. Joe leaped to his feet in time to keep the whole thing from cascading to the floor.

"That's from us." The twins each claimed a knee of hers to lean against.

DJ studied the jumping-horse wrapping paper and the tape that nearly covered it. "You wrapped it, too, huh?"

"We did good, huh?"

"You sure did."

"You want my jackknife?" Brad offered.

DJ grinned at him and ripped the paper off. Inside the box lay a Dr. Seuss book. "Hey, just what you wanted, right?"

The twins nodded. "Now you can read it to us."

"Look under." Billy lifted the book so DJ could see the T-shirt. Stormy and the butterfly graced the front.

"Oh, wow!" DJ held it up for everyone to see. Amy got the giggles, so DJ knew she must have helped the boys.

"You like it?"

"Put it on."

DJ set the box on the table and pulled the T-shirt over her head.

"Pretty." The boys spoke together as only they did so well.

DJ hugged each of them. "Thank you, guys. That's the best present ever."

"Daddy said you could sell them and get rich."

"We'll see."

By the time the table was empty, DJ had two pairs of new boots—a pair for riding and a pair for roughing it—

a new wool blazer for dress-up, new breeches, various other articles of clothing, an entire box of colored drawing pencils, and a few new CDs. Herndon had a new traveling blanket with no holes, and Gran and Joe gave DJ an etched silver cross with matching pierced earrings and a Bible.

"That's just in case you decide to pierce your ears one of these days," Gran whispered in her ear when DJ hugged her. "And I thought this new, smaller Bible might be good for traveling."

DJ had so many gifts that almost everyone had to carry something out to the car. Hugging them all good-bye, DJ felt sure she was the most blessed girl in the world.

"We'll drop you off at the train station," Joe told Sean as they loaded the car.

"Thank you, sir, but I can take the bus down there." Sean looked from DJ to her grandfather.

"No, I think not."

"You might as well give up. He won't change his mind." DJ stuffed her drawing kit in the car. "Thanks for the party at school and helping with this." She waved her arms at the whole group. "Sure fooled me."

He leaned closer. "One of these days we'll go out all by ourselves, okay?"

DJ nodded but gulped inside. *Out? As in a date? Fat chance my mother will allow that!* "See ya."

The next morning in the art room, Ms. Gant nodded and even smiled as she studied DJ's display of cards. She pointed a paint-stained fingertip at Stormy and the butterfly. "Cute. I have a niece who loves horses. How much for this one?"

"Y-you can have it."

"No, I will pay like any customer. You are an artist, and an artist is worthy of her hire."

DJ gulped. "Dollar."

"Good." Isabella dug in her pocket for a dollar bill and laid it on the table. "Thank you. Now we will talk about your career."

DJ felt her stomach drop down to her ankles. "I . . . I . . ." She took in a deep breath. "I plan to ride in the Olympics one day."

"I know that. You have been very clear on your preference for riding. But a talent like this should not be neglected, or it will wither away. That is a choice you must make."

But I'm only fifteen. DJ straightened her spine. "Why can't I do both?"

"Ah, then you agree that your art is important?" Ms. Gant leaned her back against the high drawing table and tilted her head to stare at DJ over her half glasses.

"I guess. I used to think that I just drew horses well, but now . . ." DJ studied the drawing in her hand, then looked her teacher in the eye. "Now you've made me see that it is more than that, and I don't want to let it go, either."

"I hear a *but* in your voice."

How can she know me so well? "It's a matter of time. When school starts again, there will be no time for extra art classes. My mother insists that I prepare for college, and those requirements don't leave a lot of time for art classes."

"Would you consider art school?"

"I would, but I'm not sure she will."

"Ah." Ms. Gant nodded. "Let me think on this."

7

BY FRIDAY AFTERNOON, DJ felt wrung out and dishrag-ish, but she had promised to help Brad and Jackie at an Arabian show that weekend. Jackie was waiting for her when DJ arrived at the Pleasant Hill BART station.

"So how was the rest of art school?" Jackie asked after the hellos.

"Not enough words to describe it." DJ shook her head. "I learned so much my fingers keep drawing after I fall asleep. Ms. Gant wants me to go to art school, and she even suggested the high school in San Francisco for kids who want to be artists in some way or another. She said that way I would get to try more mediums."

"And you said . . ." Jackie checked both ways before pulling out onto Treat Boulevard.

"She knows I cannot, and will not, give up my riding."

"So?"

"So I won't even think about that high school. And I'd have to talk Mom into thinking art school instead of a regular college."

"Well, the good thing there is that you have three years of high school to make that decision." They stopped for a red light.

"Not if I want to take more art classes in high school or some over at DVC like I did this summer."

"I don't get it."

"Well, if I take the college prep courses, there is very little room for more than one art class a semester. Too many requirements. Like a foreign language and more math and science classes."

"And your Saturdays are taken up with shows and your afternoons at the Academy."

"Yep."

"You are one busy girl. When do you have time to hang out, kick back?"

"Not too often."

"Well, I can't tell you how much your agreeing to do this show with us means. Both you and Amy. I feel sort of like I have the daughter I've always wanted, and maybe part of another."

"Thanks." DJ grinned at her. "I'll tell Amy she's a part of a daughter."

"No, you won't, you nutsy kid." Jackie grinned and shook her head. "Good thing we don't have far to go for this show. Davis is only about an hour away. Your things about ready?"

"Won't take long."

"Okay, I'll drop you off and go get Amy first."

They talked about the upcoming show until they pulled into DJ's circular drive. "I'll hurry," DJ said, leaping from the Land Rover and heading into the house.

"So how was your last day?" Lindy strolled in from the deck when Queenie barked a welcome to DJ.

"Great. Awesome." DJ set her portfolio case and backpack on the stairs. She drew out an envelope from the front pocket of her backpack. "Here's a letter for you from Ms. Gant. I have to rush. Jackie'll be back with Amy any minute." She gathered her things again and charged up the stairs. It would have been so easy to open the envelope and read the letter, but she'd kept herself from it. Her mother had pretty strong views on privacy.

Good thing she'd packed most of her things the night before. She stuffed underwear and a nightshirt in her duffel bag, then rolled another pair of shorts and a T-shirt and put them in. Her show clothes hung in their garment bag. At the last minute she remembered her swimsuit and then added her hair and face things last. She glanced around the room one final time to see if she needed anything else.

"Oops, a card packet." She'd promised to check with the gift shop at the horse farm hosting the show to see if they'd like to add the card line to their inventory. After all, she was drawing pictures of Arab foals. She glanced at the card on top and made a face. It was cute, but she knew how to make it even better now. Maybe she should . . . DJ shook her head and added the packet, brochure, and order forms to the front pocket of her duffel.

Ready.

Back down the stairs she charged, loaded like a pack animal. "Mom?"

"In here."

"Where are the boys?" Leaving her things by the door, DJ strolled into the living room.

"Maria took them and the neighbor boys to the movie. I was just enjoying the quiet." Lindy held up the letter. "Do you know what's in this?"

DJ shook her head. "Nope, she just handed it to me as I was leaving."

"Ms. Gant says she believes you should go to the arts high school in San Francisco starting this year in preparation for art school rather than college. Did you suggest that to her?"

"No, why would I? In fact, I told her no when she mentioned it to me. No way can I commute in there and still get in enough time in the ring." DJ slumped on the rolled arm of the sofa. "Why, what all does she say?"

Lindy looked back to the sheet of paper in her hand. "She says she believes you have been given a very great talent and that it is important for you to continue to develop this talent now and not wait until you are older. She says she would be grateful if we were to let her work with you."

"She'd be grateful?" DJ could feel her eyes grow round. She slid down on the end cushion of the sofa. "Mother, what does she mean?"

"I think she wants to be your mentor. Great artists used to do this. Maybe they still do." Lindy folded the paper back along the two lines and tucked it back in the envelope. "So how badly do you want to be an artist? I guess that is something you need to think about."

"I want to jump in the Olympics."

"Darla Jean Randall, I understand that, but unless you do something with your life to earn a living, you won't get to play with horses."

"I could make a living as an artist?"

"I don't know. This comes as a surprise to me, too." Lindy tapped the edge of the envelope on her knee. "Guess we have to do some real thinking and praying about this."

"You aren't thinking I should go to San Francisco to school, are you?" DJ shook her head as she spoke.

"I don't know what to think. Like I said, we will do some heavy-duty thinking and praying before making any decisions."

The doorbell rang, and DJ leaped to her feet. "I gotta go." She gave her mother a hug. "See you Sunday night."

While DJ caught Amy up on what was happening, the thought kept running through the back of DJ's mind that *her* mother had said there would be no decision until they prayed about it. Like heavy-duty praying. Wait till Gran heard about this. She would go through the roof.

"Stormy is waiting for you," Jackie said. "I think she's grown another inch or two since you saw her. You two are up in one of the first classes in the morning."

DJ shivered just a bit. "I've never shown a baby before."

"You've shown halter, though, right?"

"Oh yes, but just big horses. Is it any different?"

"Nope, same stuff. We'll go over this when we get there and get settled. I'll be showing in the same class as you. We think Stormy is the stronger entrant of the two, but a first and second wouldn't be bad. And it all depends on the judge's preferences."

"When is the Western part of the show?" Amy leaned forward from the backseat.

"They will most likely have two or three rings at the same time, English in one and Western in the other. Then they sprinkle the odd classes either in between or have a separate arena for Harness, Sidesaddle, Costume, those kinds of things. You and Amy will both be riding at the same time in different rings. We're going to be busy, that's for sure."

On Saturday morning Stormy was a natural show-off, just as DJ had expected. The little filly kept her head up, ears pricked forward without prompting, and when the judge came by her, she stood perfectly still, only her slightly flaring nostrils showing her excitement.

They trotted out with a blue ribbon fluttering from her halter. Once outside the ring, Stormy danced sideways, her eyes rolling a bit at the flapping ribbon.

"You are such a cutie, how could they resist you?" DJ stroked down the chestnut shoulder and smoothed the furry mane that was now beginning to grow long enough to hang over to the side. Stormy nuzzled DJ's pockets and got a carrot bit for a reward. As she munched, her dark eyes studied DJ as if trying to memorize every bit of her.

Jackie had attached her red ribbon to her filly's halter, and the four of them posed for pictures since both Amy and Brad had cameras.

"I got several of them in the ring," Amy said, snapping the lens cover back on her camera. "They were so much better behaved than the others that they would have won even if they didn't have the best confirmation."

"Jackie has spent a lot of time with them." Brad tickled Stormy's upper lip, and she nibbled on his fingers.

"You better watch out; she'll think those fingers are strange-colored carrots." Jackie patted Stormy's neck and rubbed her ears. "I love working with the babies, seeing them get used to the halter and being handled. This Stormy, she's a smart one. We do something once and she remembers, unless, of course, she's in a contrary mood. Then it's over."

"So how do you keep her in a happy mood?" DJ kept on petting her baby.

"Carrots, that's the secret. She'll do anything for carrots, like a dog will do anything for a piece of meat." Jackie glanced at her watch. "You'll have to take Stormy back out for the championship, but we better hustle. We have two up in the two-year-old filly class. It's a shame we couldn't bring the gray for the yearlings."

"He's just not growing enough to compete well," Brad said to Amy and DJ. "He'll make a good riding horse or show horse later on, but not a breeder." He led the way back to the barn. "Deej, you want to show one of the two-year-olds?"

"Sure."

At noon the English classes started, and DJ trotted into the ring more times than she cared to count. She and Amy met on the way in and out of the barn where the stablehand and Jackie groomed each horse.

At the end of the day, the ribbon board in front of Gladstone Farms had garnered a fair showing of blues and several championship rosettes.

"I've ridden more different horses today than in all my life put together." Amy rolled her head around on her shoulders and stretched it from one side to the other. The director's chairs they occupied faced the door of the tack room, and streams of people roamed the aisles outside. Jackie and Brad greeted old friends and introduced the girls, in addition to answering questions about the horses they'd brought to show.

Matadorian, Brad's principal breeding stallion, arched his neck over the doorway as if he were the official greeter. His broad, dished forehead and intelligent eyes, with a forelock that swung down on his nose, announced his fine Arabian breeding through and through. No wonder he had taken the grand champion in the Halter classes.

"You want to go back to the hotel?" Jackie asked a bit later. "I can take you over and come back. Brad wants us to meet with a very interested buyer, so we might be late."

"Sure." DJ covered a yawn with her open palm. "Sorry."

After they'd had a swim and changed into their nightshirts, DJ and Amy sat cross-legged, facing each other on the two queen-size beds in their room. They tossed the bag of chips back and forth and had to reach for the soda cans sitting on the bedside table.

"So," Amy took another swallow from her can, "tell me again what Ms. Gant wants you to do?"

"She wants me to go to high school in San Francisco—you know that one where kids who want to study any area in the arts go?"

"Like if I wanted to be a serious photographer, I could go there."

DJ looked at Amy, the thought making her bounce on the bed. "Would you?"

"I've thought about it."

"You never said anything." DJ popped another chip in her mouth.

"I know. It was more like a dream, a fantasy. There's no way my parents could afford something like that.

And besides, I'm probably not good enough."

DJ studied her friend. "Do you *really* want to be a photographer when you grow up?"

"I already am one."

"Like I'm an artist."

"Right. Besides, what if our card line really gets big? We need to get better and better at what we do to keep up with it."

DJ snagged her can and sipped. "You really think it could?"

Amy shrugged. "Seems to me it's already on the way. Like my dad says, now we've got to get smart if we want it to keep growing."

DJ studied her friend through slitted eyes. She ran her tongue over her teeth and dislodged a bit of potato chip. What if both of them went to the artsy high school? Was there a way she could get enough riding time in, too? Were both of her dreams possible?

8

"SOMEDAY I'D LIKE TO RIDE in a Costume class," DJ said Sunday morning. They were back at the show.

"Me too." Amy sighed. "He's like something out of the movies." Together they watched Brad and Matadorian sweep around the ring, full Bedouin robes billowing in the breeze. Brad's dark tan made him look almost Arabian since the white burnous cinched down by a red braided cord covered his brown hair. The tassels hanging from Matadorian's bridle and silver buckles caught the sunlight with their red and gold threads.

When the judge awarded them first place, the girls and everyone else applauded.

Later, under harness and pulling a phaeton, Matadorian flashed his way around the ring again to another blue. This time Brad wore a top hat and frock coat with a jabot so snowy it glistened. DJ and Amy met them coming out of the ring.

"You were super." DJ stroked Matadorian's nose, his flaring nostrils showing a bit of pink. "You work hard out there, don't you, fella?" The stallion nodded and snuffled DJ's hand.

"You've got him under your spell, DJ. Talk about a ham, there. Matty, old boy, she loves Herndon best, and don't you forget it."

DJ laughed. "Now if only Herndon loved me best."

"Oh, he will, one of these days. Some horses just take longer to adjust. He was that way when Jackie got him, too. He's just more businesslike."

"Snobby is what he means," DJ said to Amy, and both girls laughed.

"You guys want to learn to drive, too?" Brad lifted the reins.

"Really?"

"Sure, come on, there's room for both of you up here." Brad patted the seat beside him. "It's not much different than in the saddle, but the reins are longer." He handed DJ the reins. "Now, if you had four up, you'd thread the reins through your fingers, but with one or two, it's like riding single rein."

DJ clucked and twitched the reins as she'd seen her father do, and Matadorian walked forward with a snappy stride. She drove him back to the barn and handed the reins to Amy. "Your turn."

Amy drove them around the barns and stopped in front of their own. "Thanks, that was fun."

"Okay, now you have to unharness him and put your tack away."

DJ and Amy groaned. "Now I know why you let us drive."

"Method to my madness, huh?" Brad showed them what to do, and once the harness was off, he led the horse back to his stall. DJ and Amy wiped down the harness and then the buggy so it could be covered with a tarp and loaded into the back of the horse van.

"Okay, you girls ready?" Jackie asked when everything was loaded.

"Sure 'nough." DJ glanced around the tack room one more time just in case they left anything. She climbed in the front seat of the Land Rover and waved good-bye one last time to Brad, who drove the pickup pulling the trailer full of tack boxes, stall and tack room decorations, and the two little fillies tied in the other stall. Ramone, Brad's ranch foreman, had already pulled out with the horse van.

Both DJ and Amy fell asleep halfway home, waking up when the car stopped in front of Amy's house.

"Thank you for all your help," Jackie said, handing her an envelope.

"What's this?" Amy questioned.

"Just a little thank-you from Brad and me. This show was more fun for us than any we've done, and that was thanks to you two. We hope you can do this again sometime."

"I'd love to. Thanks." Amy tapped DJ on the shoulder. "See you at 7:30 at the barns, right?"

DJ groaned. "No. Joe is doing mornings 'cause I'm doing evenings. I get to sleep in."

"Lucky." Amy climbed out of the car and reached back in for her duffel and backpack. "See you, Jackie, and thanks again."

DJ stifled another yawn as they pulled up to her house. She should be wide awake after sleeping like she had. "Sorry we weren't better company, Jackie. Every time I get in a car lately, I fall asleep. You want to come in?"

"I think I'll head on up the road. Santa Rosa is still a couple of hours away, and I'd like to be home before midnight. At least I won't have to help unload tonight." She handed DJ an envelope, too. When DJ started to shake her head, Jackie leaned toward her. "Listen, you two worked hard for us, and if we want to give you something in return, don't look a gift horse in the mouth, okay?"

"All right, but—"

"No buts. I'll see you on Wednesday when we pick up Herndon to take him to the airport. You excited about USET camp?"

"I will be." DJ swallowed the butterflies that immediately swarmed like a hive of bees. She took a deep breath and let it out. "I had to get school and this show over first before I could think about camp."

"I wish I could stay there with you, but I know you'll have a great time. Oh, and think about that art school. There must be some way we can work it all out."

Oh man, I'd rather not just now. DJ nodded and slammed the car door. She waved as the Land Rover left her drive. Dragging her things into the house, she felt as though she could sleep for a week.

"So how did you do?" Lindy called from the living room, where she'd been snoozing on the sofa. She stretched and yawned as DJ entered the room.

"Stormy and I took a blue, and Jackie the red. I'm not even sure what all else I got, I did so many classes. Jackie and Brad let us do all the riding, other than Matadorian. You should have seen him in the Costume class. He was totally awesome."

"Your father or the horse?" Lindy brushed her hair back behind her ears.

"Both." DJ grinned. "Where's Dad?" While it still felt strange sometimes to call Robert "Dad," it was becoming more natural all the time.

"Gone to bed. He was beat." She patted the sofa beside her. "You hungry, thirsty?"

"Nope. We ate, and then Amy and I slept most of the way home."

"Sean called. I told him you'd call back tomorrow."

"Thanks." DJ leaned against the sofa back. "Showing strange horses was really fun. Not strange, you know, but different."

"I figured that out. Brad wouldn't own *strange* horses."

"Jackie asked if I was excited about USET camp, and I about freaked. Inside anyway. I didn't really want her to know."

"Why?"

"M-o-m, that camp is clear across the United States, and . . ." She paused, trying to decide what to say.

"And?" Lindy waited quietly.

"And . . . and I won't know anyone there at all."

"You'll make friends quickly."

"But . . . but what if I don't?" The words came out in a whisper.

"Ah, Darla Jean, you are always so capable that we forget sometimes you are still a girl, just barely fifteen." Lindy leaned over and pulled her daughter close. "I, for one, will miss you, and the twins are already groaning about your being gone. They asked their dad tonight who would give them their riding lessons while you were gone."

"What did he say?"

"He said you'd give them an extra one this week to make up in advance."

DJ smiled. "Good plan. Thanks a big fat bunch. Besides, I'll be gone a week."

"They haven't figured that out yet."

DJ left her head on her mother's shoulder. Lindy's perfume teased her nose and made her wonder if someday she, too, would find a perfume she liked and wear it all the time like her mother did. But for now, "eau de horse" would have to do. She turned and kissed her mother's cheek. "Night. I'm about to crash and burn."

"Tomorrow we work on cards?"

"Sure. In the morning since I don't have school. But please, please keep the boys from waking me. I finally get a chance to sleep in."

Lindy chuckled as she got to her feet. "Okay, but close your door. They were hoping you'd be home before bedtime. They've been missing you."

"And me them." DJ shook her head. "You know what? I never thought I'd think something like that?"

Lindy nodded. "Yeah, I do know, and ain't it grand?"

"DJ, wake up!"

"Go away. I'm sleeping until I wake up myself."

"Okay, but I've got some great news, and it's after ten already." Lindy sat down on the end of DJ's bed.

DJ groaned. "Go away."

"Mommy, is DJ sick?" The voice tried to whisper but failed as usual.

Queenie leaped up on the bed and stuck her cold nose into DJ's face. After a lightning-quick tongue lick, she gave a sharp, high bark.

"Sheesh, why didn't you bring General along, too?"

DJ stuck her head under the pillow.

"We'll go get him." Both boys bailed off the bed, and thundering footsteps headed for the door.

"No!" DJ threw back the covers and sat up. "You can't bring your horse up here."

"Thank you for clarifying that." Lindy leaned back, her hands clasped around a raised knee.

"I know, I have to remember sarcasm doesn't work with those two." DJ tried to glare at her mother but yawned instead. "All right, I'm awake. I thought you said you'd let me sleep all day if I wanted."

"I said that?" Lindy's grin said she remembered but wasn't admitting it. "Besides, I've got such exciting news I thought you'd want to hear it."

"It better be *really* exciting. Like we won the lottery or something."

"Well, *I* think it's exciting, and so did Robert." She rocked back and forth, her slip-on sandal flapping against her foot.

"If you don't tell me now, I'm going back to sleep."

"As if you could." Lindy pulled a letter out of her shorts pocket. "Read this."

DJ took the envelope and pulled out a letter. She read the first paragraph and threw her arms around her mother. "They want your book! Wow! They want your book."

For almost a year Lindy had talked about writing a book about young entrepreneurs, using DJ and Amy as her inspiration. Now that Lindy wasn't working anymore, she had the time to fulfill her dream.

"Well, at least they want to see more of it. Now I've got to get the proposal going, and Mom says I should look for an agent." She took the letter back and read it again. "Pretty cool, huh?"

DJ looked down where the boys and dog were rolling on the floor, laughing and barking like usual. "My mother is going to be a writer."

"*Is* a writer already. Going for author."

"Just think, Gran is an illustrator, you're a writer, and I'm an artist." DJ scrubbed her fingers through her hair.

"Such talent, huh?" Lindy patted her daughter's knee. "Maria is making strawberry waffles for brunch, so get a hustle on, okay?"

"We're hungry." At the mention of food, the boys' ears had perked up and they leaped to their feet. "Come on, DJ. We'll race you."

DJ swung her feet to the floor. "Give me twenty minutes, okay? If I don't wash my hair, it might all fall out."

The boys plowed to a stop. "You have nice hair. Don't let it fall out."

"Beat it, guys." DJ looked at her mother and shook her head. "Sheesh."

"I'll call Amy to come over, too. We've got some business to negotiate."

"What?"

"Take your shower."

DJ rushed through her shower and combed her wet hair back into a ponytail. She jogged down the stairs just as Amy rang the doorbell.

"What's up?" Amy asked. The two of them walked into the kitchen, sniffing appreciatively.

"Got me. Mom has great news—a publisher wants to see more of her young entrepreneurs book."

"Cool. Did you tell them that the showgrounds in Davis wants more of our cards?"

"Nope, forgot."

"You sit." Maria pointed at the table, decorated with a fruit plate, fresh squeezed orange juice in the good crystal glasses, and a platter of little pigs sausages. Bobby already had one sausage ready to pop into his mouth, but his father's glare stopped him.

"Grace first." Robert pulled out Lindy's chair, motioned DJ and Amy to the other side, and prayed.

"Start with juice and fruit." Maria set a waffle topped with strawberries and a ring of whipped cream in front of Lindy.

"Maria, do you want me to gain all my weight today?" Lindy speared a fresh strawberry. "Oh my."

"Baby needs food." The cook brought another plate for Robert, the mound of strawberries and whipped cream even higher than Lindy's.

"Ah, Maria, you are a saint for sure."

"So how come all this?" DJ's nod indicated the table and everything.

"Well, since you'll be leaving in a couple of days . . ."

"D-a-d, it's not like I'm going to be gone for a month or something."

"We decided to celebrate, and your mother's good news was one more reason. Besides, we have a proposal to put before the two of you."

"Us?" DJ and Amy looked at each other, then across the table.

"But first we eat." Robert raised his glass of juice. "I propose a toast."

When they all had picked up their juice glasses, he continued. "Here's a toast to DJAM, Etc. and Mom's new book. And yesterday I signed the final papers on that group of condos. May we all prosper."

"You left out General," Bobby interjected.

"And to General." Robert touched his glass to everyone's around the table. Maria set a waffle in front of Amy and grabbed Bobby's glass just before it spilled.

"And to Maria, who has the fastest reflexes in California."

DJ got the giggles, which set Amy off, which infected the boys and finally the adults so none of them could drink their juice for the toast.

After they'd finished eating and cleared the dishes away, Robert laid some papers on the table. Looking at both girls, he tapped the sheets in front of him. "This is a contract for a loan so you can have a large order of your cards printed."

"Oh, how did you know?"

"Know what?"

"The showgrounds we were at this weekend wants to order a dozen of each set for starters."

"I didn't. Your mother and I just figured this was the best thing to do to make all our lives easier. Now, here's the way it will work." He explained about the interest and the payments and answered all their questions before pushing the paper toward them. "Dad says maybe we should all buy shares in your company, but for now, this will work. One of these days you might think of hiring the residents at Outlook House to fill the packets for you. They do a good job, and it gives mentally challenged people a chance to earn some money."

DJ stared at the amount of money they were borrowing. "Guess we better sell lots of cards, huh?"

"You already have orders for more than half this amount. I'm just afraid this isn't enough." Lindy signed on the line below DJ and Amy.

"Thanks, Dad, Mom." DJ looked at both her parents. "You guys are awesome."

"Wait until your first payment comes due." Robert waggled his eyebrows. "Then we'll see what you say." He sounded like a mean bad guy—or at least he tried to.

"DJ, have you called Sean back?" Lindy asked as the two girls were leaving the room.

"Oh no, I forgot. But I will."

Several hours later, after they'd called in their big order to the printer, Amy left on her bike, and DJ dialed Sean's number on the phone in her room. Lying on the bed, kicking one foot in the air, she waited for an answer. When the answering machine clicked on, she groaned. Telephone tag again.

Time flew by as DJ's family got her ready to leave. On Wednesday she had Herndon all sheeted and ready when Brad came to pick him up.

"Do you wish you were going on the plane with us?" He slammed the tailgate in place.

"Nope. I think ours will be more comfortable."

"You're right. See you in New Jersey."

DJ nibbled her bottom lip as he drove out of the Briones parking lot. There was no backing out now—as if she'd ever given it a serious thought. Funny what things her mind did when she least expected it.

Saying good-bye to her family at the airport on Thursday was harder than she thought it would be. Not only had she never been so far away before, but this was her first flight.

"Don't worry, darlin', you'll do just fine," Gran whispered in her ear with her final hug.

"You got enough money?" Joe asked with his hug. He slipped a bill in her hand as he let her go.

"I'm so proud of you, Darla Jean, I could just pop." Lindy hugged her close.

"Not here, okay?" DJ smiled in spite of the tears she felt burning at the back of her eyes.

"You got enough money?" Robert shoved something in her pocket after he hugged her.

DJ looked from her dad to her grandfather. "Thanks, you two." She shook her head as she bent to hug the boys.

"Bye, DJ. We're missing you already." The boys each gave her a fierce hug, reluctant to let loose.

"Rows fourteen through twenty-one now boarding . . ." came over the address system.

"That's us, DJ. Let's go." Jackie put an arm around DJ's shoulders. "I promise to call you as soon as we get there." She handed DJ her backpack.

DJ looked over her shoulder as she handed the attendant her ticket.

What if something happened and she never saw them again? She stuffed the thought away and followed Jackie down the ramp.

9

LEAVING HER FAMILY BEHIND almost made DJ cry.

"You all right, DJ?" Jackie asked.

DJ swallowed and nodded. *They will all be so far away*. She stared out the plane window at the people loading luggage and food onto the plane. Other passengers found places for their carry-on luggage and took their seats. DJ had stowed her backpack under the seat in front of her. What if they lost her luggage? While her tack had gone with Herndon and Brad yesterday, all her clothes, including her boots, were in her suitcases. *I should have carried on my duffel bag*.

If all went the way it was supposed to, Brad was even now trailering Herndon from the airport to the camp facilities in New Jersey. *If all went as it was supposed to*. DJ was learning how many things could go wrong when shipping horses. Even though Herndon had flown before, they'd had to tranquilize him yesterday. He didn't like the noise or the close quarters or something.

Brad had called to say they arrived all right, but the trailer wasn't available until today.

DJ knew she shouldn't be worrying. Gran had even reminded her of her verse about the lilies of the field and the birds of the air, but still DJ chewed on her lip and wished she could get off the plane and go back home. Right now.

Instead, she pulled her small sketch pad out of her backpack, along with a couple of drawing pencils. After closing her eyes for a brief moment to remember Stormy in the show-ring, DJ began to draw the little filly as she stood at attention, her ears pricked and eyes bright. With an arch to Stormy's neck and her feet placed just so, the drawing came to life as DJ added several small lines to the whorl of hair on Stormy's chest.

DJ heard the roar of the engines change. She put her pad down to watch out the window as the plane gained ground speed. The thrust for lift-off felt remarkably similar to when Herndon flew over a fence, only this time they stayed airborne. DJ flashed Jackie a grin and gave a little wriggle in her seat. She, DJ Randall, was on her way to the East Coast—for one whole week of nothing but horses and jumping. Awesome!

"That's very good." Jackie nodded to the sketch. "I can see you're improving all the time, and I thought you were mighty good before."

"It's not done yet." DJ held up the pad. "But you can tell it's her, can't you?"

"Perfectly."

It wasn't long before DJ put the pad away, snuggled a pillow under her cheek, and leaned against the window to fall fast asleep. She slept through the meal and only woke as they approached the Philadelphia airport. They would drive from there to the Windy Bay Equestrian Center, where the camp was to be held.

DJ felt like she'd stepped into a steamy shower when they walked out to the bus that would take them to the car rental lot.

"Hot, huh?" Jackie slung her suitcase into the rack behind the driver.

"Is it always this hard to breathe? I feel like I'm sucking water." She set her backpack between her knees. "And they say it's hot in California. I don't think so." Wiping her already damp brow, she leaned back, the better to feel the draft from the air conditioner.

"If it's like this tomorrow, both Herndon and I will be dripping in two minutes."

Once in their car and on the freeway heading east, DJ marveled at how green everything was.

"Far cry from our part of the world," Jackie answered. "Guess that's why they call California the Golden State. Our hills are gold much of the year."

"I always thought they were brown or tan."

"All in the way you look at it. You hungry since you missed lunch?"

"I can eat anytime." *Even if my butterflies are fluttering. Maybe food will calm them down.*

By the time they arrived at the equestrian center, got DJ settled in, and checked on Herndon, it was already time for Brad and Jackie to leave. DJ took in a deep breath and waved again as they drove out the blacktop drive. She was on her own. *God, please help me.* She couldn't even figure out what else to ask for. Home seemed halfway around the world. DJ could hear Bridget as if she stood right beside her. *"Put a smile on your face and act as though you do this every day. Meeting new people is half the fun of being involved in the horse world. The other half is the horses."*

DJ headed for the stables—and Herndon. At least she knew him. And she was sure that horses were *more* than half of the horse world. She checked her watch; it was still half an hour to dinner. Not enough time to lunge him, let alone ride. And the woman at registration said there would be a get-acquainted meeting right after they ate.

Herndon nickered when he saw her.

"Hey, fella, how do you like your new home?" His nostrils quivered in a soundless nicker that made her want to hug him hard. DJ slipped into his stall and wrapped her arms around his neck. Resting her cheek against his neck, she breathed in the fragrance of horse, her favorite smell in the whole world. When Herndon shifted, DJ stepped back and dug a bit of horse cookie from her pocket. After he lipped it off her palm, she stroked the sides of his face and up around his ears. "Good thing I'm tall, huh, or you'd have to bend down to get the rubs you like." He blew in her face and nosed her pocket for more.

"I better go. You be good now, you hear?" As she closed the stall door behind her, she glanced to the next stall, where a girl even taller than DJ was shutting her horse's door, too. "Hi. My name's DJ Randall."

"Megan Morgan. What's your horse's name?"

"Herndon. And yours?"

"Michaelmas Days. I call him Mike." She brushed back a strand of strawberry-blond hair. "Boy, it's hot."

"And sticky." DJ pulled her T-shirt away from her body. "I'm not used to it being sticky like this."

As the two walked out of the barn, they talked about where they were from and their horses. They discovered they were in the same dorm room, which held four beds, and that they would be riding at the same time in the morning.

By the time they entered the dining room, DJ felt like she already had a friend—or at least someone to talk with. The room was pretty quiet, considering the twenty students and various adults who were seated or finding a place. DJ and Megan took chairs next to each other at a round table where two boys were already talking like old friends. They nodded when the girls sat down and went on talking.

Megan looked at her and shrugged.

As soon as all the seats were full, a man stepped up to the podium and rapped for attention. "Welcome. I am John Hamilton—please feel free to call me John. I'm glad to welcome all of you to a week of riding and schooling that will change your life. During supper it is your job to get to know the others at your table, to relax, and to get ready for the test immediately following the clearing of the tables."

DJ felt a groan inside but made no sound. Megan looked at her with raised eyebrows and shrugged.

"We'll start with these tables." He pointed to the tables closest to the food. "Help yourselves at the buffet."

After the meal, John handed out name tags along with a three-page test. "When I say begin, I want you to fill in the test as quickly as you can. There'll be no grade. This is just to help me know where all of you are. Please, no talking among yourselves. I need to know how much *you* know. Any questions?" When there were none, he said, "Okay, begin, then. Raise your hand when you are finished."

Sheesh, it's just like school, DJ thought as she began filling in the blanks. At the outline of the horse, she identified all the parts and did the same with saddles and other tack. She was feeling pretty good on the multiple choice and the vocabulary until she hit the medical section. Some of the diseases she'd never heard of, let alone their treatments. She guessed on a couple and left many blank. The last question asked what she hoped to accomplish during her week at camp. DJ tapped her pen against her teeth. The instructions to be specific made her task even more difficult.

I want to become better at being one with my horse. I want to gain confidence over a variety of jumps. She was stuck. *I want to become the best rider I can.* She left that answer because she couldn't think of anything else. She raised her hand and waited until John acknowledged her before putting it down.

When he collected the tests, he handed each of them two schedules—the daily one and one that covered the whole week and listed the different activities. "As you can see, you are divided into four groups. In the morning, two groups will be jumping and two groups will work on dressage. You'll switch in the afternoon. We've assigned you to your group based on experience, which usually groups you by age, too."

He announced a few more instructions, then asked everyone to stand and introduce themselves, including where they were from, their year in school, and the name of their horse. As they went around the room, DJ got the idea she was the youngest rider in the room. Most were seniors in high school, since this week was for the junior jumping division. She'd also traveled the farthest.

"Okay, we have make-your-own ice-cream sundaes, and then lights out at ten. Wake-up call will be at 5:30.

Get up earlier if you need more than half an hour to get ready. Any questions?"

"California girl, huh?" one of the boys said as they scooped ice cream. DJ nodded. If she remembered right, he was from Connecticut. "Bet you don't have schools like this out west."

"Nope, at least not that I know of. You been here before?"

"Third year. Let me tell you, we work here. We work hard." He passed her the hot fudge sauce.

Why do I get the feeling he thinks I can't cut it here? DJ shrugged off the feeling. She'd just have to show him and the others, that's all.

"Don't pay any attention to Kurt," Megan said on their way back to the dorms. "He thinks he's better than any of the rest of us just because he spent time training in Europe."

So would DJ get to compete against him or not? She certainly hoped so.

10

FRIDAY MORNING, FOUR GIRLS and one bathroom made for a tense half hour.

DJ figured she could take a shower later during her free time and brushed her teeth first so she could get out of there. Since there would be a room inspection later, she made a tight bed and put all her things away before heading to the barn, wrapping a scrunchie around her ponytail as she went. The sun couldn't get through the clouds on the eastern horizon, and a breeze made her shiver. It felt like rain.

She pulled two flakes of hay off the alfalfa bale and headed down the dirt aisle to Herndon's stall. He nickered and nosed her shoulder as she unlatched his stall, as if they'd been best friends for years. After tossing the hay into the hayrack, DJ stroked down his neck and rubbed his ears.

"You sure have changed your ways, big horse. You lonesome for home, too?" He rubbed his forehead against her shoulder and turned away to snag a mouthful of hay from the rack. While he ate that, DJ fetched a wheelbarrow and began cleaning the stall. Since she usually had Herndon tethered outside during this chore, she was careful not to knock him with the fork and rake. But he moved over when she asked, acting like this was an ordinary occurrence, another thing that made her grateful for his good training.

DJ poured the grain in Herndon's bucket at 6:30 sharp like the schedule said and headed for the dorm room to wash up for breakfast. John Hamilton was already talking sternly with one girl who was running late. The tone of his voice made DJ aware that she didn't want to get on his bad side.

DJ was one of the first for breakfast, so she didn't have to wait in line and was able to get through and eat quickly. She headed back to the barn to groom Herndon, hoping for time in the shower before dressing for dressage class.

"Have you already eaten?" Megan caught her coming back into the barn.

"Yep. The scrambled eggs were good." DJ patted her pocket. "Kept my banana for later."

"Just remember that you have to be doing a better-than-good job on everything. I hate getting demerits."

"I thought this was your first time here."

"It is, but I've been to other horse camps. Same drill." Megan backpedaled on her way to the dining room. "See ya in the ring."

DJ forked a pile of fresh manure out of Herndon's stall and set to grooming him, picking his hooves and braiding his mane. All the time she kept up a running conversation with his ears, answered by an occasional snort. One thing for certain, there was more horse to groom here than she'd had with Major. The thought of her old friend brought a pang of homesickness. They weren't even getting up yet at home, and here DJ was about to dress for class.

"It's weird, that's what." She flipped the sheet over his back and fastened all the straps. "Now, you stay clean, hear me?" Herndon snuffled her hair and blew in her face. "You need to brush your teeth, big horse. You've got bad breath."

DJ jogged back to her room with fifteen minutes to spare—just enough time to shower.

She even made it into the ring five minutes early, so she had extra time to warm up her horse. Herndon didn't like rushing, and so far she'd managed to avoid that.

"Oh man, look at all the mirrors!" DJ stared at the huge mirrors placed around the arena. "No wonder I don't want to compete in dressage. Hey, big horse, you get tired of looking at yourself?" Herndon shook his head, his body already thrumming like a high-voltage electric wire.

As they walked around the covered arena, what sounded like hailstones pounded on the metal roof. When they passed a door, DJ glanced outside to see lightning flash, and a few moments later thunder rolled. It wasn't hail she had heard, but huge raindrops.

Herndon flicked his ears, twitched his tail, and jigged sideways. DJ had just gotten him going straight again when another boom of thunder made him snort and settle back on his haunches, ready to jump. DJ shortened her reins and sat deeper in the saddle.

"Knock it off!" Her tone said far more than the words. With firm hands and strong legs, DJ forced him to walk forward again despite his flicking ears.

"You did well." An older woman with a whip in one

hand and a clipboard in the other entered the ring. "You folks in California don't usually get thunderstorms like this, do you?" She looked up at DJ, her blue eyes crinkled at the edges. "As you can see, horses from around here take it in stride, unless they are out in it, of course. I'm Elma Furstburg, and I'll be your dressage instructor for the week."

Even though he was standing still when the next thunder crashed, Herndon shivered and stamped one front foot. DJ stroked his neck. "I'm glad to meet you. Herndon here has competed fourth-level dressage, but I'm not anywhere near that. I've never ridden dressage in competition."

"Thank you for telling me that. But as you know, dressage work will make both you and your horse better athletes."

"That's why I do it."

"Good." The woman strode to the center of the arena and flipped on a microphone attached to her jacket. "Now that you are all here, I'll give you a few more minutes to warm up, and then we will begin." As the instructor detailed what they would cover, DJ swallowed, wishing she had spent more time with Bridget on dressage work.

The time flew by as the five riders performed all the routines Elma required. "Use your seat bones" and "Drive with your seat" seemed to be her favorite phrases, along with "More leg" and "Where are your hands?"

DJ fought her tendency to tighten her shoulders, focusing on sitting deep in the saddle, using both her seat bones. She hadn't thought of them as separate from her body before, but she did now.

By the time she'd put Herndon away and raced to the

classroom, the veterinarian who was teaching for the hour had already introduced himself.

The look on his face informed her she was late. The look on Megan's face warned DJ she'd earned a demerit.

The look Kurt gave her made her grit her teeth.

John Mark—JM as he liked to be called—a student from Georgia, strolled in behind her and sat down on DJ's right. His wink made her jaw relax, and she could listen to the vet again.

The sound of rain on the window and the drone of the man's voice combined to make DJ fight to keep her eyes open. When JM nudged her arm, her eyes flew open and she jerked awake. She glanced around, hoping no one else had noticed, but the look on the instructor's face said he had.

"You okay?" JM whispered.

"Um, I just don't know what's wrong with me."

"Time change. You're not used to being up this early."

"Oh." Of course she'd heard of jet lag. But she'd never crossed time zones like this before. DJ covered a yawn and made herself sit straighter in the chair. Slouching only made her sleepier.

"Late and sleeping, that will be two demerits." The man handed her a slip of paper. "See that you do better tomorrow."

"I'm sorry." DJ took her punishment and left the room.

"Don't let it bother you. He just gets offended if we aren't all pumped about what he has to say." JM walked beside her and glanced at his own paper before stuffing it in his pocket. "Anything with caffeine can help jump-start you in the morning."

"I was fine until I sat down in there." They stood on

the long porch of the administration building that housed the classrooms, dining room, and offices. Rain splashed in the puddles, but at least the thunder and lightning had passed over.

"This is your first time here, I take it?" His gentle drawl made her want to hear him talk more.

DJ nodded. "First time for a whole lot of things." A little bird taking a bath in the puddle made her fingers itch for her drawing pad. Next time she'd remember to put it in her backpack.

"Come on, then, let me introduce you to some of my friends." Once they started discussing horses, the time flew and the group continued talking through the dining line and at the table. While DJ didn't have a lot to contribute, she enjoyed every minute of it. As Bridget and Jackie had told her, the horse world was different on the East Coast. Most of these kids had started riding when they were five or six, if not earlier, and were used to horses that cost thirty grand or more.

DJ used her free time for a nap.

Like the dressage class, her first jumping hour drilled on the basics. Herndon had a hard time settling down, especially after another thunderstorm. They'd trotted their third time over the cavalletti when the thunder crashed right over their heads. Herndon reared and hit the ground running.

"Oh no, you don't." At least she hadn't lost her stirrups or reins. *Please, God, help.* "Whoa, big horse, come on, Herndon." His ears showed he heard her, but terror gripped his body.

They went once around the ring, and then DJ pulled him into the middle. Even when she brought him to a stop, he stood shaking. All she wanted to do was get off and walk the spaghetti out of her knees—when her heart quit hammering, that is. Instead, she stroked his neck, keeping up the gentle murmur that could calm anything but the storm raging outside.

"Are you all right?" John Hamilton stopped beside her.

DJ nodded. "He's just not used to thunder like that."

"You handled him well. Walk him around the ring now so he can loosen up again. The thunder is moving off, but that one hit right over us. Probably would have fried the barn if we didn't have lightning rods." His voice was as soothing to her as hers was to her horse.

"Thank you." DJ had admired John Hamilton for years because of his Olympic riding, but now . . . now his kindness made her admire him even more. DJ tucked the incident away to think on later. Now it was time to ride.

By the second time around the arena, Herndon was walking freely again, not feeling like a firecracker ready to explode. At Hamilton's beckon, DJ joined the class as they worked over cavalletti and low jumps.

"Timing. Timing is everything." Hamilton must have said that five hundred times by the end of the two hours.

Back at their stalls, Megan shook her head. "Man, when Herndon bolted like that—scared me almost out of my boots. Your face was as white as your shirt."

"He sure doesn't like the thunder, do you, big horse?" DJ rubbed his ears and scratched his cheeks. "I was sure John would yell at me."

"For what?" Megan unbuckled her girth.

"Losing control like that. I shoulda . . ." DJ stopped herself right there. *No more shouldas, remember?*

"Like no one else ever lost control of their horse? Get

real." Megan led her horse into his stall. "We have to groom, pick stalls, and feed before inspection at 5:30. And that means clean tack, too."

"In other words, hustle?"

"You got it."

The inspectors found sweat on Herndon's bridle, so along with her tardy and falling asleep in class, DJ now had accumulated three demerits. Two more and she would be penalized in some way. The thought of drinking coffee for breakfast looked more appealing by the minute. Surely she could get it down if she put enough cream and sugar in it or mixed it with hot chocolate. That didn't sound so bad. Now, the bridle, that was sheer carelessness on her part. A good lesson right then, but still DJ felt like a little kid being scolded by the principal.

Karen, one of the others in her dorm, had racked up five demerits and received orders to rake the barn aisles during her free time. Anyone could tell by the look on her face that she was not a happy camper.

"I don't get it," DJ said to Megan as they cleaned up for supper. "Why the demerit thing?"

"So we learn to work as a team more and build strong character traits like self-discipline, promptness, taking the best care of our horses and our gear, and paying attention. You'll hear the word *focus* until you're ready to scream."

"I already have that one branded on my hand so I can look at it often." DJ used a brush to scrub under her nails. Now that she didn't chew them, she was learning to keep them trimmed short anyway and scrubbed clean.

JM waved them to his table when they entered the dining room.

"I think he likes you," Megan whispered.

DJ could feel her neck grow warm. Not that it wasn't warm already since the sun had come out and created a steam house from all the puddles.

"Hey, it's DJ of the runaway horse." Kevin from Maine said with a laugh, his dark eyes snapping in fun.

"Yeah, and yours plowed into a fence," JM shot back.

"And then you plowed dirt," Jean, a round-faced girl from Long Island, added. She pointed to the chair between her and JM. "Sit here so we can protect you from the mighty K there."

The teasing continued through the meal, keeping everyone laughing.

When Kevin asked her what it was like in California, DJ answered, "Plenty of sun and no thunderstorms." She shook her head. "And no, not all of us are surfers."

"Ah, you trashed my dream." Kevin looked around the table. "Don't you think I'd make a great surfer dude? Show horses on the weekend and ride the waves the rest of the time?"

JM shook his head. "You have to be blond to be a surfer. That's what it says in the movies."

Kevin ran a hand through his dark, curly hair. "That and the one time I tried surfing in Hawaii, the board tried to beat me to death. I'll take a horse any day."

"Even if you can't stay on?" Megan wore an innocent look, but her eyes danced.

The movies that night were of the equestrian events from the Atlanta Olympics. John Hamilton narrated. He slowed them, reversed them, and stopped the action over and over to point out every motion of rider and horse. After a popcorn break, they went back to more movies of show jumping.

"Tomorrow night we'll review the eventing," he said as he turned off the television screen that was almost as tall as DJ. While she'd seen the videos before, never had she studied them like this.

There'll be no demerits tomorrow, she promised herself just before she fell asleep. *Please, God, no demerits.*

11

THE INSPECTORS FOUND makeup powder on the counter of their bathroom—one demerit each.

DJ felt like chewing nails. Who had time to put makeup on anyway? She thought a moment. It had to be Karen. Neither DJ nor Megan wore any, and she didn't think Selina did, either. That left DJ with one demerit to go.

"So what do we do?" DJ crossed her arms over her chest.

"You want to take her on?" asked Megan.

"We could post a sign on the mirror." DJ thought of Karen, who hadn't been too friendly to begin with. Now this.

"But it has to come down by inspection time. They don't like things like that. 'Each person is to be responsible for her own actions.'" Megan parroted the last like she was quoting from a handbook or something.

"Okay, here goes." DJ ripped a page from her notebook and wrote, "Please make sure everything is clean when you are finished." She held up the sign.

"You got any tape?"

DJ shook her head. "Sheesh, why does everything have to be so difficult?" She went in the bathroom and leaned the sign against the mirror. "There."

Sunday during their dressage class, the instructor stopped DJ and motioned her to the center of the ring. "Now, remember your aids, inside seat bone to outside hand. You don't want him to drop his shoulder. All this will help make him more supple. Do you understand?"

"I . . . I think so."

"Good. Go again."

After a few strides, Elma called again. "Now, tell me where you're tense."

"Between my shoulders." DJ's answer came immediately.

"So what will you do about that?"

DJ relaxed her shoulders and checked out the rest of her body. No wonder Herndon kept moving to the center of the ring. Her right leg was too tight, and Herndon had been well taught to move away from a strong leg.

By the end of the session, DJ was dripping wet, and not just from the humidity, either. On the way back to the administration building, she realized that today she was sweating rivers from driving a fourth-level dressage horse forward. How come it took so much to push him today, and yesterday she couldn't stop him?

After an hour's lecture, she knew more about international shipping of horses than she'd ever thought necessary. Things from papers needed for quarantine laws to finding reputable shippers. How could she ask questions when she didn't know enough to know what to ask?

At dinner Kurt told a horror story about shipping a horse to Germany. It had to be put down somewhere high above the Atlantic when, for who knows what reason, the horse went ballistic and half tore his crate apart. When the tranquilizers did no good, they had to shoot him.

"But at least the horse was well insured."

His final comment made DJ catch her breath. Was that all the horses meant to him, money?

"Easy," JM whispered from her side. "He likes to scare people, our Kurt does. Don't let him get to you."

DJ swallowed and sat back in her chair. He sure did manage to find her hot buttons—and push them. She hated to admit it, but she didn't like Kurt any better now than at the beginning of camp—less, in fact.

Her list of questions for her father was growing. He'd trained and shipped so many horses, for both himself and buyers, that he'd know how to keep them safe.

DJ had bought postcards in the equestrian center's tack shop and spent her free time writing them to her family and Amy. Though she'd called home on Saturday, the writing really made her think how much she missed them. Not that she had much time to think of anything except what was going on at camp, but still . . . She picked up the last card. Should she send one to Sean? After all, they never had gotten to talk on the phone the week before she left.

Quickly she drew the head of a foal up in the left-hand corner. Then she wrote, *No drawing time here, but I'm learning lots. DJ.* She checked in her notebook for his address and added the stamp. Dropping them in the mailbox, she headed for the swimming pool, where most of the rest of the campers splashed and played.

On Monday John Hamilton raised the bars on the low jumps up to two and a half feet and then up to three feet so they could no longer just pop over them. Now they were really jumping.

And DJ kept getting left behind again.

"It's all in the timing, DJ," Hamilton said. "You've done it before, you'll do it again. Now, focus and count the rhythm. Trust your horse."

Sure, trust my horse and go sailing by myself when he quits. DJ knew that Herndon wasn't trusting her, either. His hesitation showed it.

When the horse in front of them quit, Herndon quit, too, and so did the one behind them.

"Okay." Hamilton shook his head laughing. "This is getting to be contagious. You are all trying too hard and tightening up. Relax. Come on, shoulders, neck, back, hips, legs, arms, and hands." As he named each body part, he moved his to show them how he wanted them to move. "You cannot jump your best when you are tight. If you're tight, your horse will be, too. Horses are incredibly able to pick up your tension. Now, on the rail and trot. Concentrate on relaxing."

"At least it's not just us," DJ said to Herndon's flicking ears. He snorted as if he totally agreed.

That night when they watched the videos of the day's work, DJ recognized right when she tightened up. The suppleness went out of her, and her arch over Herndon's withers wasn't there. Therefore, he wasn't rounded, either.

The next afternoon she did much better.

"So what's the difference?" Hamilton asked.

"I relaxed. My grandmother always says if you smile, you relax. Yesterday I wasn't smiling—and I *really* wasn't relaxed."

"You're not behind today, either, are you?"

She shook her head. "The video of me taught me a lot." *And seeing it on a big screen like that helped, too.* She knew that if she asked for a large-screen television, it would appear, but her family had given her so much already.

"I hate to ask for things." Back in the stall, Herndon nodded and nosed her hand. She gave him the horse cookie she'd kept in the grooming bucket and stroked his neck while he munched. Of course, it took someone good on the camera to get the shots so she could see what she did. Maybe Brad could do that for her, or Joe.

At least she hadn't gotten any more demerits.

"So, DJ, how has the week gone for you?" John Hamilton joined her at the cold drinks machine Wednesday afternoon.

"G-great."

"You have a minute to talk?"

Do I have a minute? Does the sun get up in the East? "Sure."

"What kind do you want?" He motioned to the machine, his coins at the ready.

"Uh, root beer." The can clunked down and he fished

it out to hand to her. "Thanks."

He got one for himself and, popping the top, stepped off the porch. "How about over there?" She kept pace with him, sipping her soda and wishing she could think of a way to tell him how the week *really* had been for her.

"What do you plan to do with what you've been learning?"

"Jump in the Olympics." The words came out before she could think.

"You're sure."

"Have been for years. That's my goal and my prayer. So far God has given me what I needed." *Now, why did I say that? Duh.*

"Me too. I wondered from the way you acted if maybe you were a Christian."

She wanted to ask how, but she sipped her drink instead.

"You have a great horse for where you are."

"I know." *Should I tell him?* "Herndon's a gift." She went on to tell him about Major and the injury, about Brad and Jackie and the rest of her family and the Academy. "Bridget Sommersby is my trainer."

"I read that on your application. She had high praise for you, and from her, that is something. I competed against her more than once, and I've wondered where she had gone to." He sipped and shook his head. "Amazing the way lives touch and then somehow touch again." By now they were sitting on an oak glider under a maple tree. "Tell her hello for me, will you?"

"Sure. Why don't you come do a clinic for us sometime at Briones Riding Academy? That's Bridget's school." *Why would you ever say that? Hello?*

"Sounds like fun. I like California, just rarely get out

there anymore. Tell her to contact me." He turned a bit so he could watch her. "So . . . what could keep you from your dream of the USET?"

"Me, mostly, I guess. I know it's terribly expensive, too, but if God wants me there, I'll be there. My family says they'll do whatever we need to do to get me there. And I have my own business. That might help, too."

"You do?"

"My friend Amy and I have a line of cards with pictures of horses, mostly foals, on them. I draw, and Amy is a photographer."

"Really? Would you send me a sample? Do you think they'd go well in our store here?"

"I don't know why not. They do well in other tack shops." DJ leaned against the back of the seat. "Somehow I need to fit in both art and riding . . . because I think God has given me gifts in both areas, and I don't want to waste anything He gives."

John nodded. "The two areas might not both peak at the same time, but one can't ride twenty-four hours a day, seven days a week. Sometimes getting to the top is easier if a person is one-tracked but it seems to me that people who have balance and a love of beauty fare better in life. Go for it, DJ. Go for it all. And if there is ever a way I can help you, please let me know."

"I . . . I will."

"And I'll see you back here next year?"

" 'If it's up to me, it will be.' " DJ quoted a sign that hung in the classroom.

"Good." He stood and held out his hand. DJ shook it and nodded. Then she grinned up at him.

"And I sure hope I see my cards in your shop. They're better than postcards, more like frameable art."

His shout of laughter made her grin wider.

"John?" Someone called from the administration building.

"I gotta go. Thanks for talking with me." He smiled again and headed across the grass.

DJ watched him go. "God, I don't know how you did this, but thanks a whole heapin' bunch." Instead of going directly into the dining room, where most of the campers had gathered, DJ dogtrotted over to her dorm, took out her notebook, and wrote down everything she could remember that John had said, and what she'd said, too. Then she went to join the party.

Their last classes were Thursday, as was the jumping competition.

At the end of the dressage hour, Elma handed each of her students a list of suggestions for further improvement. She also added comments about their strengths:

You are a willing pupil and follow directions well. I see great things ahead for you. Elma Furstburg.

DJ looked up to smile at her teacher. "Thank you."

"You're welcome. I hope to see you back here again next year—a lot more proficient in dressage."

"I will be more proficient whether I come or not. I need to be the best athlete I can, and so does Herndon."

"You have the right attitude." Ms. Furstburg moved on to the next pupil.

With each event of the day, DJ thought, *Last time, this is the last time*. Though the big one was still coming up.

But even anticipating the jump-off paled next to her

talk with John the day before.

"Okay, this is the way we will do this," Hamilton announced after the noon dinner hour. "The five members of group A will jump first, followed by B, and so on. The top two in each group will go for the next jump-off. There will be jump-offs in each group until there are two remaining. Riders will be eliminated as in any jumping ring; rules remain the same as in any jumping competition. Only if the two finalists tie more than two rounds will there be a timer added. Any questions?" When no one said a word, he waved his hand. "Dismissed to prepare. Full jumping attire."

On one hand, DJ was grateful to be in the first group, but on the other, she had less time to prepare. But Herndon was as ready as he would ever be, groomed to the last shine. DJ's tack gleamed, as did her boots, and her black jacket and white breeches hung on their hangers. The sooner she loosened Herndon up, the better.

"You ready?" Megan pulled her second boot snug.

"As I'll ever be." DJ picked up her helmet. "Let's do it."

Promptly at two, all the instructors gathered in the announcer's box at the outdoor jumping ring. Some spectators sat in the stands, the ingate and outgate keepers stood ready, and assistants leaned against the fence to replace any fallen rails.

Having drawn number one, DJ jumped first. She circled the practice ring a final time and trotted forward when the ingate keeper swung the gate open. "Okay, big horse, this is it. All we have to do is our best." Herndon pricked his ears forward, broke into a perfect tempo canter, and cleared the post and rail with ease. After the stone wall, he swished his tail as if this were child's play.

The in and out loomed ahead, but as DJ counted *three, two, one,* and they catapulted into the air, she wanted to shout her joy.

He cleared the brush with a foot to spare and snorted as they exited the ring.

DJ gave Megan a thumbs-up as she trotted toward the opening gate. While Megan jumped a clean round, their three other classmates didn't fare so well. Group B began.

Two winners came out of that group without a jump-off, but both the third and fourth groups had three jumpers with clean rounds. JM and Kurt were the finalists in their group.

"We will let the finalists of the A group lead off," Hamilton announced. "The jumps have been raised six inches. DJ Randall is riding Herndon."

Herndon snorted as they neared the ingate. DJ felt like giggling. This was so much *fun*! And judging by the smile she felt on her face, DJ was as relaxed as ever.

Their round showed it. Nary a nick.

"That a way." JM rode up beside her. "You two were having a party out there."

At the end, five campers were still in the running.

"The jumps will be raised another six inches." The assistants hustled to raise them all and within minutes gave the thumbs-up signal.

"DJ Randall on Herndon."

The gate swung open and they were back in the ring. "Okay, big horse, let's party." Lift-off on the airplane didn't compare to the way Herndon pushed off for each jump. And the touchdown was much lighter. DJ rode out of the ring to the audience's applause. Again, a clean round.

Four made it.

Kurt, JM, Kevin, and DJ faced jumps three inches higher.

"You're up with the big time now." Megan had put her horse away and hollered from the sidelines.

DJ swallowed hard. For the first time that day, her butterflies were performing aerial routines—in formation. Would they help lift Herndon and her over the jumps?

She heard the crack on the next-to-last jump. When the audience groaned as they leaped the final jump, she knew her pole had hit the dirt. "But we did our best, big horse, we did our best." Kevin jumped after her, and he, too, heard the fatal crack. His pole didn't even wobble but clattered to the ground.

Kurt rode past her with military precision, his face set in total concentration.

JM smiled at DJ and kept his horse moving in the practice ring. "Wish us luck."

"Oh, I do."

JM and his horse flying over the jumps was pure poetry in motion. The lift-offs and touchdowns looked as easy as an afternoon canter. They jumped a clean round.

Kurt trotted into the ring, picking up a canter, with perfect rhythm.

DJ shared a glance with Megan, who wrinkled her nose. Chuckling to herself, DJ watched Kurt approach the stone wall. *Three, two, one* . . . The horse hesitated, then with a curious twist, lifted over on sheer guts with only a whisker of clearance.

A group sigh told of everyone's relief.

Kurt brought his horse around and headed for the

wall again, this time clearing it, but with no change in his expression.

"Makes me wonder if he really likes to jump." Megan leaned on the fence by DJ.

The bars went up another three inches.

This time JM ticked on the in and out. The bar wobbled.

DJ held her breath.

The bar stayed in place as JM aimed for the chicken coop. He went over again, and before DJ could catch her breath, he was cantering out of the ring, patting his horse's neck all the way back to DJ.

"Oh man, what a way to spend an afternoon." He pumped one arm. "Yes!" He turned in his saddle. "Go, Kurt!"

"He's rushing them." DJ hated to say what she was seeing. "Come on, Kurt, take it easy."

The highest bar on the in and out toppled. Kurt finished his round to applause and cheering, but he rode out of the ring without acknowledging them.

"And our winner for today is John Mark Hanlin on Once Again of Peachtree, Georgia. Second place goes to Kurt Schwartz on Sidor from Greenleaf, Connecticut. Let's give an extra round of applause for our two winners and all the entrants."

DJ cheered and clapped with the rest. As far as she was concerned, by far the best man had won.

"You'll each have pictures of taking the brush jump. They'll be in your packets when you leave tomorrow. But I'd like the four finalists to enter the ring now for a group photo."

DJ reentered the ring to stand next to Kevin. "You did good."

"You too," he answered. "A newbie showing up lots of returnees. Good for you. Won't be long until we see your name on the winners' lists."

"Hope so." She smiled for the camera and gave Herndon a hug.

Trotting out of the gate, she thought ahead. Tomorrow they would fly home, and early Saturday morning they'd drive to Rancho de Equus for the show. It couldn't get any better than this, could it?

John Hamilton led the final lecture on Thursday night, titling it "The Olympic Mind-set."

DJ thought he must have sat down with Gran, Joe, and Bridget to discuss how to help Darla Jean Randall the most. He talked about the importance of dedication, not just to physical perfection like perfect jumps and the greatest horse, but to building the kind of character that could win or lose with grace, that kept on trying when all the chips were down, and that knew how to be a team player as well as a leader.

"You must learn to do your very best, and then, win or lose, let it go. Let it go! Look to the next jump, the next test, the next event. Not just for the Olympics but for life. There are a lot of losers out there who whine and blame someone else, anything else, but you . . ." He looked each of them right in the eyes. "You know that when you have done your best and given it all you have, you have won, be it in the ring, in the boardroom, or in your home. The medal isn't the proof of a win. Doing your best is. I'm proud to know winners like you."

DJ clapped with the others, wishing she had some better way to show her appreciation for all he had done for her that week. *Just do your best, that's all you can do.* She had another show coming up to prove it.

12

FOG AND THUNDERSTORMS could really mess up air travel.

So DJ found out. Between the thunderstorms on the East Coast that delayed their leaving and the fog on the West Coast that wouldn't let them land, DJ arrived home a day late, feeling like someone had pulled the plug on her energy and enthusiasm. If only she could go to bed, she knew she would sleep around the clock.

Brad met them at the gate. "I've got Herndon in the trailer, and I've already talked with your mother. The others have gone on to the show, as you well know. Joe said he would come back and get you, but I told him I'd just take you on, if that's all right with you."

"I guess." *That means I won't even get a shower before I go.* She felt her hair. Stringy like it hadn't seen water for a week. *All I want to do is go home.*

"Our luggage is at carousel D," Jackie said with a sigh. She and Brad had vacationed in Maine while DJ was at the USET camp, then returned to take her and her horse home. She laid an arm over DJ's shoulders. "At least you slept part of the way on the plane. If that baby hadn't been crying so loud, I'd have slept, too."

DJ rubbed her ear. "I think I caught his earache. If I could only pop this thing . . ."

"Try holding your nose and blowing. That's what a stewardess told me one time."

DJ did that but shook her head. "Nada." She forced a yawn, but that didn't work, either.

"Maybe if we get you something to eat and drink, that will help." Brad had steered them to join the flow of people toward the baggage area.

DJ stretched her jaw again and tried yawning with a hand cupped over her stubborn ear.

"Want some Tylenol or something?" Jackie stood behind DJ on the moving walkway.

DJ swallowed repeatedly but with no letup in the pressure on her ear. Instead, the pain was intensifying, giving her a bad headache. She'd never had such an earache before.

The wait to pick up their luggage seemed hours long.

"Look, DJ, you can miss this horse show if you want." Brad looked at her and shook his head. "You look like a ghost, and with your tan, that's hard."

"No, I'll go. This will quit pretty soon, and after I sleep, I'll be fine. Bridget really wanted me to show in this one because of the judge. He doesn't usually come out to the West Coast, and Bridget's planned a dinner for us all at the end of it. I can't let her down over a silly plugged-up ear." She pulled on her earlobe, feeling more like banging her head on the wall.

When they finally had all their luggage, they loaded it on a cart and pushed it out to the Land Rover Brad had driven over from long-term parking.

"Thank you for helping us," Jackie said with a sigh

as she sank into the leather seat and leaned her head back on the headrest. "What a trip!"

DJ buckled her seat belt and rubbed her ear. If only the thing would pop. She opened her mouth wider and wider, but while it made her yawn, it didn't help the pressure that had turned to pain. No wonder that baby had been screaming. She felt like doing the same now.

"Thanks." Gratefully she took the Tylenol Jackie handed her and slugged them down with water from the proffered bottle.

They let Brad out at the truck and trailer parked in the enclosed lot by the transport company. Herndon nickered when he saw them and shifted in the double horse trailer. DJ wished he'd nicker for her again, but so far that hadn't happened. So far a lot of things hadn't happened yet—especially her earache going away. *Please, pills, work fast.*

Taking the front seat when Brad got in the other rig, DJ watched the scenery as they turned south on Highway 101. If plans had gone right, she and Herndon would have had a day of rest at home before setting out for the show again. And as Gran often said, "If wishes were horses, beggars would ride." Her stomach began to feel queasy at the stop-and-go traffic on the multilane freeway. One more thing to contend with.

"So," Jackie asked after the traffic let up some, "what would you say is the most important thing you learned at the camp?"

DJ didn't need to think on that one at all. "That there are lots of kids out there with the same dream I have, and if I ever want a spot on the Olympic team, I have to be the best rider and have the greatest horse. We watched videos of past Olympics, and the final jump-off is always a killer."

"Do you still want to do it?"

"More than ever." DJ kept her hand over her ear. That seemed to give a bit of relief.

"Is the pain better?"

"A little." She didn't mention her upset stomach and headache.

Two long hours later, as the day turned to dusk, they drove into the horse park at Rancho de Equus. Since the show had officially started the day before, they drove right to the barn housing the group from Briones and parked in the parking lot.

DJ felt dizzy when she got out of the car and leaned against it to wait for the world to stop spinning.

"DJ, are you really all right?" Jackie came around the front of the vehicle and put her hands on DJ's shoulders. "I think we should just take you home."

"No." DJ didn't shake her head, but she put all the force she could muster into the word. "I'll be all right once this ear lets up and I lie down for a while." Everything in her screamed, *Yes, take me home. I need my mother*.

A veterinarian met them before they had Herndon unloaded. He checked the horse over and scanned the papers Brad handed him. "Okay, you can take him in. I see you are scheduled for a stall in barn D, over there." He pointed to a low building off from the others.

"I was told the Briones Academy group was in barn A, right here."

The man checked his sheet again. "They are, but since you are coming in so late, they ran out of stalls. I think there was some kind of mix-up. You aren't the only ones in that other barn, and the stalls are every bit as good."

"Who's in charge?" DJ could tell by the clipped tone of Brad's voice that he was put out. The tightness of his jaw said the same thing. "Fine, we'll leave the horse in the trailer until I get this straightened out. Jackie, you and DJ go on in and see how everyone is doing. DJ looks like she needs to sit down."

"Or lie down," Jackie added.

When they walked into the Briones Riding Academy area, only Tony was there. He turned from talking to the kids in the next tack room when he saw DJ coming.

"Man, you look terrible. What's wrong?"

"Gee, thanks." She tried to smile, but any movement in her face hurt. "You know where Joe is?"

"They all went to dinner. DJ, you better sit down before you fall down. What happened?" He set out one of the director's chairs for her.

"Her ear plugged up on the flight home," explained Jackie, "and the pain is excruciating. She thought if she could lie down for a while . . ."

"That happened to me once. Had to go to the doctor." Tony leaned down to look DJ in the face. "Did you try a hot washcloth? That sometimes helps."

"No, we came right here." Jackie laid her hand on DJ's shoulder. "Maybe we should take you to urgent care. There must be a clinic around here somewhere." She looked up at Tony. "What happened with the stalls, anyway?"

Tony shook his head, a disgusted look on his face. "They ran out of stalls, and since we had an extra, they took over ours. They said we could have it back tomorrow, so if you can bear that stall in the other barn for tonight, tomorrow you'll be here with the rest of us."

"I don't care." DJ kept her eyes closed. "Just so Herndon has a safe and clean place and I get a bed pretty quick."

"I'm sleeping in Joe's camper, and all you ladies are in the motor home. Bunny's suggestion. Hope that's all right?"

"I don't care." It was all DJ could do to keep from crying. Why wouldn't her ear pop so she could feel all right? *God, please, this hurts so much, please make it quit.*

Tony glanced at his watch. "They should be back soon. DJ, you better go to the doctor so you can get over this right away."

"That does it." Jackie straightened. "DJ, you stay right there. I'm going to find us some help." She left the tack room and turned right. A minute later Brad came from the other direction.

"Nothing I can do about the stall tonight, so I put Herndon out there, fed him, and made sure he had hay and water. There are several other horses stabled out there, too, but it's plain Jane, not like in here. Where's Jackie?"

"Gone to see about some help for DJ." Tony squatted down in front of her. "You could lie on the tack box."

"Right."

"DJ, do you want to go back out to the Land Rover? You could lay the seat back."

"No." Even talking hurt.

Brad stood behind her and with gentle fingers began rubbing her neck and shoulders. At first even that hurt, but within minutes DJ could feel her shoulders get warm and begin to relax.

"You've got magic fingers."

"Hmm?" He leaned forward to hear her.

"I said you've got magic fingers." Talking with clenched teeth wasn't easy.

"I wish." He stopped when Jackie entered the tack area. "What'd you find out?"

"There's an urgent care clinic about a mile from here, and I just called them. They said to come right in, so that's what we'll do." With each of them putting a hand under DJ's arms, they half lifted her to her feet and walked her back down the aisle to the car.

DJ had no will to resist. All she could think of was getting rid of the pain.

"Have you had a cold lately?" the doctor asked when he saw her a few minutes later.

"No. I had the sniffles a couple of days ago, but that went away right away." DJ swallowed when he told her to and kept herself from flinching when he put the otoscope in her ear.

"Um, just as I thought. Inflammation." He checked her neck and nodded again. "Okay, are there any medications you are allergic to?"

"N-no. I'm never sick."

"Okay, we'll give you an antibiotic and a decongestant/antihistamine, and here's a sample of some new pain pills. Sometimes if someone has had a cold or sinus drainage and then flies, the ear plugs up and you get severe pain, especially if you don't chew gum or you happen to fall asleep. But I can almost promise you will feel better by morning. Heat on the ear tonight can help, too."

"Good."

"She's entered in the horse show over at the Rancho. Do you think she can ride in the morning?" Jackie asked.

"Depends on how she feels. If you are at all dizzy, I would forgo the show, but you might be feeling so much better that you can participate."

By the time they got back to the grounds, the others had returned from dinner, and Bunny showed them the way to her motor home. "You take the bunk bed there, and Hilary can sleep on the pullout." Bunny folded the cover back. "If you need anything, let me know. And we promise to be quiet when we come in."

Jackie came in with a warm washcloth when DJ was in bed and helped her put it under her ear. "You need some help getting undressed?"

"Oh, that feels better." DJ almost shook her head. "I'll get undressed later."

"Most likely those pain pills he gave you helped, too." Jackie held out a glass of water and two tablets from the prescriptions they'd stopped for.

"I keep thinking Brad and I should get a hotel room and stay here for the night in case you need to go home."

"Mm." DJ heard her as if from a long distance. Her eyes felt like someone was stitching them closed. "Thanks."

DJ had no idea when she woke up, but glancing out the window, she could still see the moon hanging on the tops of the trees. DJ turned over and tried to go back to sleep, but her eyes that had been so heavy earlier now had springs on them.

Thirsty. I've got to get a drink. She eased out of bed, halfway surprised she still had her clothes on, and tiptoed to the bathroom right across the narrow hall. She cupped her hands under the faucet and, after satisfying her thirst, splashed some on her face.

I don't hurt. The thought caught DJ by surprise. She swallowed, and while her ear was still plugged, the pain was so minor she could hardly notice it. The doctor had been right. Trying not to make a sound, DJ crawled back in bed and closed her eyes. Now she could really sleep.

But sometime later she gave up. *I'll go check on Herndon*. Again easing from the bed, DJ picked up her shoes and a jacket and, guided by the light coming in the windows, made her way to the door. Since her eyes were now accustomed to the dark, she found the door handle and slowly, so as not to make a squeak, opened the door and stepped outside.

A cool breeze sent the hairs on her arms standing at attention. She shivered. Maybe she should just go back to bed. But then she remembered the time change. Her body was used to getting up at 5:00 A.M. Eastern time, and that would be right about now.

The damp from the grass soaked her socks, so DJ stopped long enough to put her shoes on. She stretched and sucked in a deep breath.

Smoke . . . did she smell smoke? DJ sniffed again. Who would be burning anything at this time of night?

13

HOW TO FIND BARN D.

DJ threaded her way through the vehicles, using light from the moon and the tall posts that held yellow-toned lights. She felt like a burglar must, trying to be quiet, trying to find the valuables in a dark house or building.

A giggle almost grabbed her. What would her mother say if she knew her daughter was running around the showgrounds in the middle of the night, checking on her horse?

"She'd probably have a whole lot to say," DJ spoke aloud, albeit in a whisper. Hearing a voice, even if it was her own, was strangely comforting. Why did she have this need to see Herndon? It wasn't as if he was Major, after all. She wished she'd been paying more attention when they arrived yesterday, but the pain in her ear had made that impossible.

She crossed the graveled area to the barn set back from the others. Sniffing, she wondered again who could be burning something in the middle of the night like this. "Maybe someone who doesn't want the pollution control people down on them." Again, talking aloud made her feel not quite so alone. One year when Gran had started to burn some wood trimmings in their yard, some official had come to the house and told her to put it out.

DJ pushed back the door, and a cloud of smoke rolled over her. Fire! Where was the light switch? The fire alarm? "Herndon!" She screamed his name and ducked back outside to breathe.

A whinny came from the far right of the barn. She called his name again, and the same whinny responded. *Get him out of there!* Taking a deep breath, DJ stepped back inside the barn, feeling along the wall for the light switch. Where was it? She ducked back outside, coughed on the smoke, took in a deep breath, and screamed, "Fire!"

Was there anyone to hear her? Where was the night watchman?

Other horses were whinnying and nickering in fear. How would she find Herndon's stall?

When DJ stepped back inside the barn, she fumbled on the wall again and found the fire alarm. She jerked the handle down and saw a bright light down at the right end of the barn. Flames! Fire!

"Oh, God, help me." She could hear someone screaming like she always did when she saw fire. It sounded like a child. "God, please!" *I can't freeze now. The horses, what about the horses?*

Her eyes refused to leave the flickering lights that seemed to be growing with each breath she took.

Herndon whinnied again, the fear in his call shattering the glass bell that seemed to hold her in one place.

DJ dove into the interior of the barn, using the light from the fire to guide her. She ran down the aisle, coughing, her eyes burning. Herndon whinnied again and banged against the wall.

By the firelight DJ found his door latch and threw it open. Her eyes streamed so bad from the smoke, she felt like she was trying to see underwater. "Come on, fella, we gotta get out of here."

Herndon pressed against the back of the stall, snorting and wild-eyed. He reared, striking out with one front foot.

"Easy, boy, it's just me. Come on, you gotta behave." DJ kept her eyes from the flames she could now hear roaring. Her eyes burned, her throat burned. She coughed and felt for the lead shank that always hung beside the door. With it in her hand, she kept up a gentle murmur between choking coughs. Herndon stopped shifting around and reached out with his nose, a nicker coming through the smoke. DJ grasped his halter and, snapping the lead shank in place, backed toward the door.

Herndon planted his feet and shrieked in fear.

DJ remembered learning that horses are so afraid of fire they will die in their stalls rather than leave what they thought was a safe place.

Without another thought, DJ dropped the lead shank and whipped off her jacket. She folded it and tied it around Herndon's eyes. Then jerking again on the lead shank, she led him out of the barn, even managing to pull him into a trot.

She could hear fire sirens in the distance. A man ran up shouting. DJ handed him Herndon's lead rope, whipped the jacket from his eyes, and before the man could grab her, darted back inside the barn. This time she ran down the aisle, flinging open the stall doors as she went. As she neared the fire, the horse in the last stall was screaming in terror.

Please, God, please, God. While she couldn't say the words around the coughing and her burning throat, DJ's mind screamed for her. She grabbed the lead shank and entered the stall, talking gently with what air she had. When she could grab the horse's halter, she snapped on the lead shank, tied the jacket over its eyes, and led the animal out of the barn.

"Here." She shoved the lead shank at a person standing there and repeated her actions, again dodging the hands that reached out to stop her. She brought out another horse. By this time the fire crew was driving in. Horses screamed their fear and agony. People were shouting.

DJ headed back for the barn.

Somehow she managed to twist away when someone tried to stop her. All she could think was to get the horses out.

She could hear others doing the same as she was. Turning to the right again, DJ paused long enough to listen for a screaming horse. *Another down this way.* She fumbled for the lead shank and darted into a stall.

Get the horse out. Don't think about the heat. DJ doubled over coughing but managed to get the lead on the horse anyway. Jacket on its eyes, it followed DJ to the barn door. The horse reared, and DJ felt herself going up in the air with it. When her feet touched ground again, she jerked on the lead shank and started forward again.

This time the horse bolted. Its shoulder caught DJ in the back and slammed her against the doorway. *Stars . . . you really do see stars.* Blackness engulfed her.

14

"GOD, PLEASE LET HER LIVE. Please don't take DJ home to be with you, I beg you, please."

Who's talking? DJ heard the voice, but where she floated, the fog didn't let her see.

The barn! The fire! Is Herndon okay? Please, can you hear me?

She floated off again.

The lights were so bright. Was it still the fire? DJ tried to swallow but gagged instead. Something was in her throat, her burning throat. She tried to open her eyes, move her hands. Did nothing work?

"I think she's coming around."

Now, who was that? She felt a cool hand on her arm.

"Darla Jean, darlin', can you hear me?"

Gran. Gran is here. Gran, tell them I can't move. With every bit of focus and concentration she had, DJ blinked her eyes and forced them open again. She could see. Gran's beloved face swam through the tears that leaked out of DJ's eyes.

"Hello, darlin', I knew you'd come back."

Where have I been? Why can't I talk? What is this thing

in my throat? How come my hands don't move?

"You're in the hospital, darlin', been here for five days."

DJ realized it was pain she felt in her hands and head. What had happened?

"You were injured in the fire at the barn at Rancho de Equus. Thanks to you, all the horses were saved."

A pain like nothing she'd ever known descended, smothering her like the billowing clouds of smoke. Gran's voice faded away.

Each time DJ regained consciousness, she learned a little more of the story. They thought the last horse she'd been trying to save knocked her into the wall and ran over her. A kick in the head had sent her into a coma. DJ's hands were tied down to keep her from pulling out the tube in her throat that led to the ventilator that helped her breathe. Inhaling as much smoke as she had was terribly hard on lung tissue.

Her family took turns coming to see her. Was there something they weren't telling her?

When they finally took the tube out, she croaked, "How's Herndon?"

"He's fine. He's still spooky, but Jackie and Brad took him back up to their ranch to care for him until you get back on your feet." Lindy laid a hand on DJ's arm. "You just rest and let your body heal."

"So what's wrong with me?" The words were hard to hear, even coming from her own mouth.

"Well, you lost a lot of your hair in the fire." Lindy glanced at DJ's hands. "It was a miracle the fire fighters found you. Some man kept screaming about that little girl that kept bringing out the horses. He saved your life."

"I'm not very little." *So things had been bad back there, huh? I almost died.* The thought didn't seem to matter much right now.

"Darla Jean, you've been in a coma for almost five days."

"Oh." *From the fire? No, that's right, I was kicked in the head. Stupid horse, I was just trying to save its life.*

Her eyes drifted closed again. *Sheesh, you'd think I've slept enough. . . .*

Joe was beside her when she woke again.

"Hi, GJ." Frogs croaked better than she did.

"Hi, yourself. I was about to shake you to make sure you started to pay attention."

Were those tears in his eyes? She oughta know about tears. Her eyes seemed to leak nonstop. DJ thought awhile. Should she ask him?

"Joe, is there something they aren't telling me?"

"Not sure."

She could tell he was hedging. *There is something more.*

He took in a deep breath and let it out slowly. "You might have some side effects from all this. They're not sure yet how long you will be dizzy from the blow to your head."

She heard an *and* at the end of his sentence. "Okay. So?"

"And your hands were badly burned."

"Oh." *So how bad is badly?* The fog rolled in again, and she slipped back into la-la land.

DJ seemed to live on waves of pain. They'd ebb for a

bit, then come crashing back like the monster waves in Hawaii she'd heard about. But each time, the intensity lessened and she woke again more quickly.

Robert sat in the chair beside her bed, soft snores coming from his slack lips.

DJ tried to stifle a groan, but her moving woke him.

"Can I get you something, DJ?"

"Water." He held a straw to her lips, and she sucked down the cool liquid. "Ah, thanks." The croak had drowned.

"How ya feeling?"

"Not very good. When do I get to go home?"

"Got me." He propped his elbows on the bed. "Probably when you can walk some. They had you out of bed yet?"

"Nope. What time is it?"

"It's 3:00 in the morning."

"How come you're here?"

"In case you need something, like water."

"Oh. What day is it?"

"Saturday."

"Where's Mom?"

"Sleeping at the hotel."

DJ thought a minute longer. "What hospital am I in?"

"UC San Francisco. They have a special burn unit. The doctors figured this would be best for you."

"Oh." She knew she sounded like a total dumbbell.

"There have been articles about you in the newspapers. You're a hero, you know."

"Why?"

"Saving the horses."

Something that had been bothering her hovered at the edge of her mind but refused to come forward and be recognized. "Humph." *Is it something to do with the fire?* She wished she could remember.

When she woke again, Gran sat in the chair, her Bible in her lap, her lips moving in prayer. "Hi, Gran. You and God got it all worked out?"

"I don't know about me, but He surely does. How're you feelin'?"

"Cruddy." At least breathing didn't hurt so badly now. If it wasn't for the pain in her hands . . . When the doctors and nurses worked with them, DJ passed out screaming every time. She took in another breath. "Water, please."

After drinking, she looked her grandmother in the eyes. "Tell me how bad my hands are."

"Ah, darlin', I'd hoped you'd wait on that, but . . ." She sighed. "Okay, there will be some skin grafting."

"What does that mean?"

"They take skin from an unburned part of your body and apply it to the burned areas."

"Oh. What else?"

"There will be a lot of physical therapy to restore the strength and range of motion in your hands."

"How long are we talking about? Days, weeks?"

"Months."

The word fell like a rock in the middle of a pond, sending waves out from around it.

"Months?" The pain crashed in on her again, and she felt as if she were drowning.

Later, sitting on the edge of the bed sent the world into spin formation. When DJ opened her eyes again, she smiled at the giant stuffed panda bear sitting in the corner, holding a bouquet of bobbing Mylar balloons.

"That's from everyone at the Academy." Lindy sat beside her daughter on the edge of the bed.

"Cool." DJ let out a breath and wrinkled her forehead. What had felt like a terrible sunburn was gone. She was making some progress. "Okay, so now we walk, right?"

"Yes, over to that chair." The nurse motioned to a chair about three feet away.

"That's all?"

"We'll talk after you make that."

Even with both of them supporting her, DJ sank down on the chair with a sigh of relief. How could she ever be so weak? At least the room stayed in the correct position, no spinning. But pulling air into her injured lungs was still hard. The nose prongs for oxygen had become her good friends, not something to fight.

Sunday afternoon after a morning of wanting to scream at the pain and the doctors and life in general, DJ woke to find Gran again in the chair.

"So you're back." Gran's smile seemed to glow in the light coming from the window.

"Uh-huh. This morning was real bad." DJ looked at her hands. At least the bandages were smaller. Maybe that was a step in the right direction.

"Gran, answer me truth."

"If I can." She kept her finger tucked in her Bible to keep her place.

"Am I going to ride again?"

"I don't know why not."

DJ crumpled back against her pillows. "No one will answer me when I ask. They just say, 'wait and see.' I don't think the doctors think I can. Gran, I can't live without riding."

"It will take some time and a lot of work on your part."

"I can do that."

"I know."

DJ thought some more. "I keep seeing the fire again. But you know what? I don't hear that kid screaming anymore."

"I'd say that's part of the miracle."

"What miracle?"

"Darla Jean, darlin' girl, you got all those horses out of a burning building. There was fire there, and you went in anyway!"

"Oh. You're right." DJ squinted her eyes. "I remember standing at the door. I couldn't go in. The child was screaming. But then I heard Herndon whinny. I could hear how terrified he was. So I went in."

"And got him and several other horses out, plus screamed fire and sounded the alarm. I'd say God answered our prayers."

"You mean about the fear thing?"

"Uh-huh." Gran stroked down DJ's arm with a gentle hand.

"Couldn't He think of an easier way?" DJ blurted out the words before thinking.

Gran laughed her gentle, loving laugh that brought a smile to DJ's face. "I don't presume to know the mind of God, darlin', but I do know that He turns evil to good for those who love Him."

"So you think I can quit scaring little kids at their birthday parties?"

"I have no doubt."

"That would be good." DJ sighed again.

This time when DJ fell asleep, instead of fire, she dreamed of clearing jumps with crowds screaming to cheer her on. She and the other members of the USET stood on the podium waiting for the officials to drape the gold medal ribbons around their necks.

No matter how long it took, she *would* ride again.

Early Teen Fiction Series From
Bethany House Publishers
(Ages 11–14)

———⊶⊷———

BETWEEN TWO FLAGS • by Lee Roddy
Join Gideon, Emily, and Nat as they face the struggles
of growing up during the Civil War.

THE ALLISON CHRONICLES • by Melody Carlson
Follow along as Allison O'Brian, the daughter of a
famous 1940s movie star, searches for the truth about
her past and the love of a family.

HIGH HURDLES • by Lauraine Snelling
Show jumper DJ Randall strives to defy the odds and
achieve her dream of winning Olympic Gold.

SUMMERHILL SECRETS • by Beverly Lewis
Fun-loving Merry Hanson encounters mystery and
excitement in Pennsylvania's Amish country.

THE TIME NAVIGATORS • by Gilbert Morris
Travel back in time with Danny and Dixie as they
explore unforgettable moments in history.